WITHDRAWN

SKIN
DEEP

E. M. CRANE

DELACORTE PRESS

Published by Delacorte Press
an imprint of Random House Children's Books
a division of Random House, Inc.
New York

Delacorte Press and colophon are registered trademarks
of Random House, Inc.

Visit us on the Web! www.randomhouse.com/teens
Educators and librarians, for a variety of teaching tools,
visit us at www.randomhouse.com/teachers

Library of Congress Cataloging-in-Publication Data
Crane, E. M.
    Skin deep / E. M. Crane. — 1st ed.
      p. cm.
    Summary: When sixteen-year-old Andrea Anderson begins caring for a
sick neighbor's dog, she learns a lot about life, death, pottery, friendship,
hope, and love.
    ISBN: 978-0-385-73479-0 (hardcover)
    ISBN: 978-0-385-90477-3 (library binding)
[1. Coming of age—Fiction. 2. Death—Fiction. 3. Self-confidence—Fiction.
4. Dogs—Fiction. 5. Interpersonal relations—Fiction.
6. Friendship—Fiction.]   I. Title.
    PZ7.C8484Sk 2008   [Fic]—dc22   2007015121

The text of this book is set in 11.5-point Janson Text.
Book design by Vikki Sheatsley

Printed in the United States of America
10 9 8 7 6 5 4 3 2 1
First Edition

For my family,
especially Mark and Wyoma Anne

SKIN
DEEP

ACT
1

1 My name is Andrea.

My locker is the fourth one down from Mrs. Donough's room. She's the teacher they call the Doughnut.

The Doughnut teaches earth science and I think she's all right, but I guess you can't be a fat teacher with a last name like Donough and get off easy. If you look like adorable little Kimberlee Dorcus, with her tiny sweaters and lip-glossed mouth, not too many people will call you the Dork because of your last name. But the Doughnut isn't cute and perky. Kimberlee is.

Actually, I consider myself lucky not to have a horrible last name. It's Anderson. Andrea Anderson. If I had a last name like Beagle or Dumley, I'd be screwed. There are kids with ugly faces or bad skin, annoying personalities or fat thighs. There's the girl with the receding chin that makes her nose look like a ski jump. The boy with bad breath. These are the kids who learn to keep to the edges, to hide.

Then there's that other category of kids. The Desirables. *Them.*

I am definitely not one of them. I am plainish, boring, nervous. Average student. No school activities. Andrea Anderson, a Nothing. I just am.

It's better to know where one falls in the social stratosphere, and I fall somewhere between Too Lame to Invite to a Party and Too Ugly to Go Out With. I move through the halls of school as if I'm not really there. The hallways between classes are like the stage in the school auditorium. There are actors performing roles from different plays, not noticing that a million other performances are going on at the same time. Simmonsville High School Presents: Act 1—Cheerleader Ashley Gets Bad Haircut and Cries. Act 2—Psycho Tries to Make Crystal Meth in Science Lab. Act 3—Future Valedictorian Accused of Cheating on History Test. Some acts, naturally, are accompanied by predictable choreography. And it's the choreography of the Cheerleaders I'm watching from my locker: they are huddled around Cheerleader Ashley-with-Bad-Haircut's locker. Ashley-with-Bad-Haircut dabs at tear-stained cheeks in a tiny locker mirror.

"It'll grow back, honey," Teena Santucci is saying, running her jewel-color fingernails through her own glossy hair. Teena wears a diamond-studded bar through her navel that makes me shudder because it had to hurt, didn't it?

The Doughnut sticks her lightbulb head out her door. She looks right through me to the Cheerleaders and sighs.

"Okay, ladies, get to homeroom."

Ashley-with-Bad-Haircut frantically repairs her makeup as the Cheerleaders drift away.

"The bell hasn't even rung yet, Mrs. Donough," Teena mouths off, but she's already heading down the hall. The Doughnut ignores her and pulls her big head back into her classroom.

The bell rings, and it's just me and sniffling Ashley in the hall. Ashley grabs a notebook from her locker. She

4

slams it shut. She sees me looking at her and looks back, not smiling.

"Tell me the truth," she says.

Her eyes are red-rimmed, outlined with gray eyeliner. Her face and neck are flushed and pretty, like she's just dashed back to the sidelines from the center of the basketball court. She's wearing a blue kilt and a tight baby-doll T-shirt just concealing her stomach.

Her hair isn't so bad, I decide. But I hesitate to tell her. If I say it looks okay, she'll think I'm kissing up. If I say it's horrible, she'll think I'm a jerk.

"About my hair," she says when I don't answer right away. She points to her head as if I'm stupid. What used to be a sleek ponytail is now a short bob, gelled to stick out here and there. Tousled.

"I guess it matters more how *you* like it, not how I like it," I say, shrugging.

"Well, I hate it," she barks.

I shrug again and shut my locker.

"Doesn't make a difference to me either way," I say.

Ashley doesn't respond. I notice from the corner of my eye that she's still standing there, facing me.

I look up.

Ashley's face is registering surprise. She blinks hard at me. I wonder briefly if she's angry.

"Oh, it's so stupid," she laughs suddenly. "You know, when I was seven, my brother cut my hair. Snipped my bangs back so far it looked like the first two inches of my forehead had been shaved.

"Took months for it to grow back. Every kid in the

neighborhood called me Forehead. I survived it, and I'll survive the jackasses who make fun of me today."

Ashley flicks her hair with cherry-red fingernails and heads for her homeroom.

"It's not like I have a choice, do I?" she whispers as she passes me. I'm surprised by how confiding her voice sounds. Like maybe she thinks *I matter*.

2 Homeroom with Mr. Diego.

Mr. Diego wears consignment store clothes and forgets to trim his ear hair. He whispers things like *"Carpe diem"* as forlorn homeroom students trudge in. Or he glares at us from his big metal desk.

It depends on the day.

Today he's glaring. The nerdy kid next to me whispers that Mr. Diego needs drugs for manic depression. I smile and the nerdy kid's face floods with relief, as if he's grateful. That's one thing about high school I've learned—even when you're unnoticed, there's usually someone else with a more painful role than loneliness. Girls who get their bras snapped in gym class, boys who endure a fist squashing their brown-bag lunches in the cafeteria. Both noticed and hated. Sometimes that's a solace, to not be one of them.

In homeroom with Mr. Diego, the students sit in alphabetical order. I'm in the first row, last seat. Diego does roll call: Allessandro, Almand, Amman, *Anderson*. Two football players copy someone else's homework next to me. Nicole Belloff is digging a pack of gum free from her overstuffed purse.

"Nicole, you just dropped a tampon on the floor," one of the football players says. Nicole frantically dives for her purse, groping beneath her chair. The football players both burst out laughing, and Nicole shoots them a dark look.

"Works every time, brother," laughs one football player. The pair high-five each other, then look around the room with gloomy boredom.

A few stragglers come in and take their seats.

"The bell rang eight minutes ago." Mr. Diego's voice is icy. The room gets quiet, but we all know Mr. Diego won't do anything. No one really gets to his homeroom right on time. Sure enough, he sighs and continues roll call.

"Carson, *Muriel*. Carson, *Peter*. Chistaldo. Chow."

"Purina Dog Chow!" hoots a football player.

Same joke, different day.

3 I walk in the woods.

I do it before Mom comes home from work, so she won't snarl at me from the other end of her TV remote, demanding to know if it's safe for a teenage girl to walk in the woods alone. In the woods, I feel safe. Nothing makes me self-conscious. I can sit on a fallen tree and watch the water rush over the creek stones like tiny rapids, or contemplate things like how deer make their own system of passages through the dense underbrush.

I take the trailhead from the top of our cul-de-sac. First, there's a wooden plank over a culvert, probably placed there by some since-grown-up neighborhood kids. It's not too sturdy, but it serves its purpose. Then there's a forgotten farm field that's overgrown with burdock and sumac; a clutching, scratching barrier protecting a row of elderly trees at the far end of that field. Just when I'm tired of getting my arms bloody and my legs whipped by all sorts of field grasses, I step into an abruptly different landscape: beaten-earth paths cushioned with a carpet of rotting leaves. Hundreds of smooth gray trunks of beech trees. Deeply creased oaks. I can hear the rushing creek water in a ravine below. Where the creek has swollen in springtime and deposited soft, soaked soil, there's a huge garden of weeds and flowers. Sometimes I startle a deer or even a fox.

I've asked for a dog every Christmas and birthday since I can remember. For a while, I rounded up Mrs. Leahy's old Labrador next door for my walks. But Mrs. Leahy didn't like how muddy the dog came back, and when she had to pick masses of burrs free from the Lab's fur, she kindly told me to leave the dog home.

Every Sunday the newspaper advertises a Dog of the Week. It's a homeless dog living on Death Row in the local animal shelter, and there's a black-and-white picture of the doomed, with its name and description below: *Bucky. Great with kids. House-trained. Lovable personality.*

"Someone gave old Bucky up for a reason," Mom would say. "He probably eats couches for a hobby." My hand, eagerly holding the newspaper page for my mother's review, would drop. Rejected again.

So, I walk in the woods alone. Sometimes I imagine a loose-skinned basset hound or a silky golden retriever, running, occasionally coming close enough for a reassuring pat on the head.

The walks in the woods save me. There I'm not invisible by the choice of others. I'm not plain, or boring, or nervous. I'm not judged by the trees, the creek, or the earth.

There's this TV show Mom watches every night during dinner.

It's a comedy, with a single mom raising four teenagers. Crazy things happen, like the car keys disappear for three days, or one of the teenagers has a new boyfriend who picks his nose and wipes it on the furniture. Every episode, this stupid TV family is thrown into an uproar, but it always manages to get in group hugs for good measure by the time Mom finishes her microwave dinner.

Mom and I sit on the old couch and set our soda cans on the coffee table. We only talk during commercials, Mom's rule. Then we have three minutes of advertising for Iron Supplements for Aging Adults over which to discuss our lives.

"School okay?"

"Uh-huh."

"Did you get the mail?"

Sometimes Mom asks if I'm going to join something. Hang out at school more. I shrug and say nothing.

"For God's sake, Andrea, you're a sophomore. Aren't you into *anything* yet?"

My face burns. I know Mom is just trying to play the role of *Mom*, and it will pass. I only have to wait for the commercial to end and she'll be absorbed in her TV show again. When the show's over, she'll forget to question my life. She'll move on to stacking dishes in the dishwasher or throwing her hideous hospital cafeteria uniform in the wash, and I'll go do my homework.

My favorite teacher is this wisecracking hippie guy who runs the biology lab. His name is Mr. Ferris. There's something safe about the way he walks around the lab, beaten-up Earth Shoes shuffling on the too-shiny floors, as he smiles and encourages us. The football players in my lab call him Fag Feet and the Desirable Girls curl their lips in disgust. Mr. Ferris doesn't even acknowledge the squeals of horror or the airborne frogs in the back of the lab. He just keeps smiling.

After doing my homework, I read. I read just about anything I can get my hands on. Tonight it's *Perilous*, a romance book from Mom's bedside table about a woman plotting the murder of her lover. It's the same random type of reading I do in the orthodontist's waiting room, where they have every breed of teen pimple magazine and you can't help grabbing one because it's better than staring around a room full of fellow metal-mouths.

I read in bed, mostly. I have a little reading light that clips onto the headboard. My bed is pushed against the window. I have posters on my walls that I keep meaning to take down. My little alarm clock radio is set on a plastic plant table next to my bed, and I've placed pens and pencils in the crevices on top of it. There are a closet and a dresser, both still stuffed with the toys and clothes of a kid of around six.

I don't remember being unhappy when I was six. I had

friends, or really playmates, I guess. There's a difference. A playmate sticks around when there's something fun to do. A friend sticks around even when there's nothing fun going on.

Victor Rizzo is the closest thing I've ever had to a friend. Mean kids called him Fat Boy. We walked to baseball practice together, both grumbling about how neither of us was very good. It was with Victor that I first started walking in the woods. We invented games where we were great explorers, or Indians, or sorcerers. It was natural for us to make up imaginary worlds to live in for a few hours on a Saturday afternoon.

Victor kept an ant farm in his bedroom. It was two sheets of Plexiglas, joined on all sides with narrow strips of wood. There was a hole in one of the wood strips, plugged with a rubber stopper. Victor could pry out the stopper to add water, or small bits of stale bread.

Inside the farm, hundreds of ants had built intricate passageways in the dirt—a microcosmic society where they worked, ate, and rested. As Victor and I watched through the Plexiglas, the ants developed a functional culture in a space the length of a sheet of paper, the width of a deck of cards. They were oblivious to the giant people watching them.

Sometimes Victor wanted to shake them. I knew he wanted to watch as their perfectly ordered world capsized beneath clots of dirt, to see their frenzied, vain attempts to reorganize until the shaking stopped and the dazed survivors emerged from the rubble to rebuild.

Victor did it once, shook them. I screamed. His father had charged into the bedroom.

13

"For crissakes, stop being the God of the Ants," Victor's dad shouted. "They're just ants. You're supposed to learn from them, not kill them. It's a damn science project."

Since then, I've never been able to think about God for too long without coming to the conclusion that humans are just someone's science project. That the galaxy is just someone's Plexiglas box through which to view the futility of human existence.

And resist the urge to shake.

Sleep doesn't usually come for a while. I position my pillow so I can see out my window, to the hopeful pools of light cast on neighbors' porches. The alarm sounds in the morning shortly after Mom's car door slams and the car starts, not too energetically. Then it's time to shower for school.

Back to homeroom.

Where it all begins again.

5 Mom is home.

She complains about the weather as she tears the plastic film from her microwave dinner.

"I got you a job today," she says.

I twitch with dread.

"You know that old house on the hill down the road?" Mom continues, punching buttons on the microwave. "The one that needs a coat of paint?"

I don't say anything, but I know the house she means. The house is at least two hundred years old and sits on top of a hill, with a winding gravel driveway lined by wrought-iron fences. It has huge, dark windows and an ancient cement swimming pool near the road. For as long as I've been around, the pool has never been used. It's filled with dark rainwater, leaves, sticks, and who knows what else.

"Mrs. Menapace is in the hospital," Mom says. "She'll be there about a week. Gloria told me she lives alone. Since we're all neighbors, Gloria and I stopped by her room to see if she needed anything."

Gloria is Mom's friend. Gloria lives one block away, and I suspect the only reason she and Mom stopped by Mrs. Menapace's hospital room was curiosity. No one knows much of anything about Mrs. Menapace, and knowing things is my mother's main thrill in life.

"Anyway, Mrs. Menapace said she has a dog in the

15

house, and she was very upset that no one could go feed it. I told her you'd feed it and let it out twice a day while she's in the hospital."

"I'll take care of it," I finally say. Mom says nothing. She removes her dinner from the microwave and goes into the living room to watch her TV shows.

Roger Dupris and his friends are shooting hoops in his driveway a few houses down from Mrs. Menapace's house. It's a cool evening, and I can see their breath as they chase each other around the driveway after the basketball, hurling insults and laughing. Roger is a good athlete and hangs out with other good athletes. They're the serious ones, the ones who believe hard work will get them slick college scholarships.

Ever since we were little kids, Roger has waved to me from his yard. He still does it, for some reason. I think it's weird, but it must just be a mix of habit and good manners. I always wave back awkwardly. Tonight I'm relieved when none of his friends notice this exchange. If they did, I'm sure they'd say something nasty to me, or tease Roger. *Who's that, your ugly girlfriend?* Roger knows I'm a Nothing, but acts like he doesn't care. I'm grateful for that.

Wendy Cartwright lives next door to Mrs. Menapace, in a split-level ranch that looks out of place next to the old Victorian. Wendy isn't outside, but her little brother Paul is in the driveway fiddling with the wheels on his skateboard. He watches me walk up the gravel driveway to Mrs. Menapace's house, his mouth half open like he's about to shout a warning.

16

I climb the dozens of steep stairs cut into the hillside to reach the front door.

It's locked. Of course.

There's a muffled thump on the other side of the door, and I almost jump out of my skin. Then I hear a hoarse, deep bark. Just one bark, not a frenzy of barking, and I stand there wondering how to get in, and how come no one even knew Mrs. Menapace had a dog, and just how big is this dog anyway?

I turn around and look toward the street. I can see rooftops and the cement swimming pool that probably hasn't been used in a hundred years, and even Roger Dupris and his friends, still playing basketball. I've never viewed my neighborhood from this height, and it makes me feel like I'm somewhere I shouldn't be. Then there's another thump at the door and I remind myself that I'm allowed to be here, and I should probably feed the dog before it eats the front door.

There's a narrow dirt path leading to Mrs. Menapace's backyard. I follow the path, curious about the old lady who can't keep up with her house repairs and has no friends to watch her dog.

The backyard is fenced in. There's a gate, crowded by a bushy mass of vines with fragile teacup-flowers. It's unlocked.

6 Once, when I was a little kid, my dad took me to a park in New York City.

I remember us standing there, my hand clasped inside his. I remember kaleidoscope gardens and perfect lawns, clipped bushes and shiny-legged park benches. I was awed. The flowers were planted in patterns, and I had knelt down on the grass and focused on just one single petal. I concentrated on tiny veins and subtle indents in its surface. Then I let my eyes glaze over. The edges of vivid color grew fuzzy. It was blissful. It made me feel the way I did those times before Dad left, when he took me to Foster's Ice Cream Shoppe and lifted me to look through the glass case at the barrels of ice cream. The colors of ice cream, lined up one after another in frosty silver buckets, was almost unbearably inviting.

There in the garden in New York, Dad had gathered me in his arms and whispered in my ear.

"All these beautiful colors," he'd said in his lazy way, stubbly cheek pressed to mine.

"Yes" was all I could say.

"If Nature made all these flowers look the same, it would be a boring garden. It's all the different kinds that make it so beautiful."

I had nodded at his solemn face. Before he let go of me, he gave me a soft kiss on the eyebrow.

"Just you remember, people are like that, too. Just like that."

That was the last day I spent with Dad.

Now, standing at the threshold of Mrs. Menapace's backyard, I remember that day with my dad with such clarity, it makes me gasp.

Mrs. Menapace's backyard is a massive garden, divided by narrow walkways and stone walls only as tall as my shins. There are raised limestone planters, arranged in a diamond pattern. There's a weathered statue where the centermost diamond points come together, surrounded by neatly piled rocks. There are strands of ivy, white and green, sprawling over the rocks and reaching up the legs of the statue. A statue of a naked man.

It's early spring, and the gardens are at different stages of coming alive. There's a blaze of tulips beyond the herb garden, arranged in a semicircle around a stone bench with curlicue designs on its seat. They aren't neatly arranged like the garden in New York City, but tightly packed and wildly colored, fire orange and dusky purple. Crowding above them is a row of lilac trees, budding flowers on slender branches.

I follow the stone path.

Between the stones, there's some sort of herb growing with tiny blue-purple flowers. Beyond the row of lilacs, I can see massive clots of dormant rosebushes and another stone statue, this one of a woman. She's also naked, lifting a baby from between her legs. Somehow, the image isn't disturbing; it's gentle.

There are massive ceramic urns at the center of the

19

rosebushes full of black dirt, but no flowers. Another park bench, and beyond it more empty raised plant beds, stone walkways, all leading to a beginning-to-turn-green lawn, surrounded by gnarly apple trees.

The main path leads to a huge back porch beneath a heavy roof. The steps leading onto the porch are smooth, like beach stones.

From the back, Mrs. Menapace's house is magnificent. The long windows appear different on this side, almost friendly, and I notice there's some gingerbread woodworking up near the steeply angled roof. When I reach the porch, I turn to look out over the gardens and smile.

I like this garden more than the one in New York City. I like it for being unruly instead of perfect.

At the back door there's a muffled bark; this time it sounds less unfriendly. I figure if anyone can get torn to shreds by challenging a strange dog on the threshold of its own home, it might as well be me. But when I turn the door handle, there's no dog baring its teeth in my nervous face.

It isn't there at all. I hear dog toenails trotting across wood floors somewhere inside, away from me and the back door.

I don't know its name.

I stand in the doorway for what must be a full minute, wondering what to do. I know I have to go in at some point, but I had been hoping to meet the dog outdoors so it wouldn't mistake me for some drugged-out, confused kid looking for something to steal to support my habit. Dogs hate intruders, especially those who show up after the master has been carted off on a stretcher the day before.

With my luck, it was probably a Doberman or a Rottweiler.

"Here, boy."

Or girl.

"Here, boy, come on outside and go to the bathroom." I'm using a ridiculous singsong voice, like I'm a brainless teenager from one of Mom's TV shows. I think of Roger Dupris down the street shooting baskets with his friends, and hope they don't hear my screams of agony as I get torn to shreds by a pit bull or timber wolf. It would be embarrassing to be known around school as the girl who got mauled to death by an old lady's pet.

There's a soft whine from down the hall, followed by the sound of something getting nudged, like a pantry door or cabinet.

"Hungry, boy?"

The fact that this still unseen dog has chosen to show me where to get its food, rather than eat me, gives me courage. I step inside the hallway and wait for my eyes to adjust to the dusky light.

I'm standing in a formal sitting room. Velvet curtains like in a movie theater are draped heavily over the windows. There are three elegant sofas covered in thick velvet, silky pillows thrown haphazardly on each. There's an Oriental carpet, a bit worn out. A marble fireplace, paintings on the wall in heavily ornamented frames. It reminds me of either a funeral home or a room in a museum.

Near the window there's a huge easel, and beside it a table covered with paint containers and mixing trays, paintbrushes scattered around and submerged in dainty teacups. As my eyes adjust more, I notice there's a clothesline pinned to the ceiling, drooping with the weight of a sheet of paper.

I begin to walk over to what must be a painting, but I'm stopped by a pitiful moaning in the kitchen.

"I'm coming," I say.

To my right is a narrow hallway, lined with drawers that are built right into the walls. Beyond that, I can see into an old-fashioned kitchen, washed dishes in a wooden drying rack on the counter.

Still no dog.

My footsteps sound hesitant on the floor as I walk into the kitchen. If he wanted to maul me, he would have done it by now, right?

I cross the threshold into the kitchen, just as the dog whacks its own head against a cupboard door.

I muffle a scream behind my fist.

The dog isn't a dog after all. Not like a terrier, or even like Mrs. Leahy's Lab. No. This dog is a horse. Its legs look as thick as my own. Its back is huge and muscular, and then there's this boxy head, on top of a neck as big as my waist.

The dog is brown and white, with odd patches of black fur. When it turns to look at me, its eyes are masked like a raccoon's. The stripe between its eyes gets broader at the top of its head, and there's a brown patch of fur, almost round, at the very center of its forehead.

"Holy Jesus," I say to the dog.

The dog, now fully aware I'm not his mistress or anything remotely like her, doesn't seem alarmed. It walks across the kitchen floor and places an oversized paw in a metal food pan, sending it clattering across the floor.

I'm reminded of Ashley-with-Bad-Haircut, pointing to her own head to illustrate her point.

Yeah, I'm hungry, stupid, so feed me.

I don't hesitate any longer. I quickly find the bag of dog food in the cupboard, try to pick it up and realize it's too heavy to lift, so I go and get the dog's food dish and dip it in the dog food bag. I pull out a pile of kibble.

The dog is patient. Its eyes don't register any unfamiliarity with me. I set the dish down, and it waits for me to back away before approaching it.

"Hope she didn't think you were gonna be a watchdog," I say, still using that goofy TV sitcom voice.

The dog inhales the food, its powerful jaws frothing. When it's done, it belches, shakes its massive head, and heads for the back door.

I had left the door open. By the time I reach it, the dog is already trotting to the grass. It squats, and I assume it's a girl.

"Holy Jesus," I breathe again, but this time with relief. If things were going to go south on this little adventure, I probably would already be half-buried in the backyard by that huge thing. After a few seconds of sniffing around, the dog trots back to the porch and into the house.

That's when I notice the huge puddle of pee on the edge of the parlor carpet. I squeeze past the dog, shut the back door behind me, and leave the puddle just where it is.

7 Mr. Diego is like a storm cloud brewing the next morning, his black eyebrows pursed together like he's just smelled something bad and can't figure out where it's coming from.

He spits our last names out: *Almand, Amman, Anderson,* like each of us is a type of venereal disease. I see that the football players are going to get a rare shot of Diego's venom.

So does the nerd sitting next to me.

"Watch this," the nerd says in a low, giddy voice. "Diego's gonna eat them up. This whole thing is about to turn into a bad horror flick."

I don't smile. The rage is boiling up red from Diego's too-tight necktie. The football players are propping textbooks over their crotches and making kissing sounds at Nicole Belloff.

"Mr. Chistaldo and Mr. Cromwell." Diego's tone is enough to stop Hayley Carter from pushing back her cuticles.

There's an awkward silence while we all wait for what comes next. Usually, in these outbursts, Diego slams his hand on his crappy desk and shouts something like *Let this be a lesson to all of you. Look at these ungrateful students wasting their education to become future lawn boys or bartenders.* The football players snigger as we all endure their punishment.

But today Diego allows us all to notice him for a moment. We wait for his sputtering rage.

It doesn't come.

Instead, Diego stands up and laughs. He laughs. Then he begins removing his tie, and we all sit in silent bewilderment.

With a flourish, Diego allows the tie to slip between his fingers to the floor.

"That's it, ladies and gentlemen," he says softly. "I quit."

The first bell rings as Diego walks out the door. Still bewildered, we all give him a moment to leave before we head to class.

After fifth period I have study hall in the library. It drives the librarian, Mrs. Nettlemoyer, crazy that she has to allow the overflow of study hall students into her library instead of stowing us safely away in a monitored classroom where we belong. I always sit in the same cubicle, mostly because it's a cubicle, with little walls on three sides to protect me from everyone around me.

For biology I'm supposed to complete this dumb worksheet showing photosynthesis, and I give it a halfhearted try while I listen to two kids making out in the cubicle next to me. I don't recognize the girl's voice when she instructs her partner to open a textbook in case anyone comes over. They giggle between kisses, and I wonder how you can be so intimate with someone as to look them in the eyes after you kiss them. I figure the first time I kiss someone, if that's ever, I'll kiss them and then run away so I don't have to let them see my eyes right after.

Finally, I can't stand it anymore. Mrs. Nettlemoyer is perched on a stool over her CHECK OUT BOOKS HERE! sign, her knees even with the table that holds her computer and coffee mug.

No one's near her table, but I approach her like she might suddenly shout at me to be quiet in the library. Instead, she lifts her face from her computer monitor and smiles like I'm some sort of paying customer.

"Yes?"

"Where would I find books about dogs?"

"Could you be more specific, dear?"

"Different breeds. With pictures." I'm grateful she's at least being nice.

She taps on her keyboard for a moment, looking up dog books. It's then that I have a horrifying thought: what if she leads me to the books, and everyone sees me following along behind the librarian, and then she announces, too loud, *"Dog books are right there, dear."* No doubt there are people in the room who would start barking at me.

"Here," she says. "Huntington, Donald, author. *Illustrated Book of Purebred Dogs*, title. It's right on the shelf across from us."

She points without getting up, and I'm flooded with relief. I find the book quickly and return to my study cubicle the long way around so I don't have to go past the Making-Out Neighbors.

Mrs. Menapace's dog is on page forty-seven in the chapter titled "Giant Breeds." *Saint Bernard. Can weigh over two hundred pounds. Gentle giants, if well treated. Formerly used for mountain rescue.*

26

I'm disappointed when the bell rings and it's time for social studies. I leave the book in the study cubicle and allow myself to be carried away by the stream of students in the hallway. Act 4—Jock Runs Fingers Down Back of Unsuspecting Goody Girl. Act 3—Goth Cell Phone Rings; Goth Tells Mom to Go to Hell.

And then there's me: Act 2—Preparing for Encounter with Saint Bernard.

It's Friday, and the school bus ride home is more rambunctious than usual. Even Frankie Seymour, who never talks to me, leans over the back of his seat to pass on the news.

"You're in Diego's homeroom, aren't you?"

I ponder the tone of his question for a second before answering.

"Yeah."

"An ambulance came to school and got him today," Frankie says. "Turns out he had a gun in the teachers' bathroom and shot himself."

It's moments like this that bond kids of all backgrounds together. The Desirables suddenly speak to the Undesirables, and while Frankie is just a freshman and has no real status yet, he manages to gather a group of unlikely comrades in a huddle around my bus seat.

"I didn't know," I say dumbly.

Wendy Cartwright is among the faces, and though she and I haven't spoken since the fifth grade, she begins asking me about a hundred questions. More faces appear, each looking at me, each interested in what I must be about to reveal.

It's their air of expectation that makes me freeze up. I really don't know anything.

"Everybody thinks he's a total jackass in homeroom, that's all I know," I say, my voice a squeak. The crowd of faces instantly crumbles into lack of interest and disappears. Only Frankie remains peering at me over the seat.

He looks disappointed in me.

8 Fridays after school, I go grocery shopping. I do it on Tuesdays, too, because I can't carry enough stuff in the two oversized canvas bags I sling for the six-block walk from Gimelli's Shop and Run. Mom says it's good exercise, but I feel stupid carting home damp boxes of Lean Cuisine and microwave pizzas when she could just drive me there when she gets home. Luckily, no one ever notices me walking along with these two bags like pontoons jutting out from my sides.

Gimelli's Shop and Run has dirty light fixtures. Mrs. Gimelli runs the cash register. She's fat and wears peasant dresses and hollers at her husband behind the meat counter. The Gimellis stock Italian delicacies that I like to look at, olives and pesto sauce and seasoned meats. Mr. Gimelli pretends to have a hearing problem when Mrs. Gimelli talks.

"They geraniums." She is holding a meaty paw at the window when I walk into the Shop and Run. "They need the watering, Johnny."

Mr. Gimelli salutes people who walk into his store. Today he's stocking the cardboard candy bar boxes near the cash register.

"They get the watering when I tell them they get the watering," Mr. Gimelli mutters with a wink at me.

I get four boxes of hamburger macaroni Lean Cuisine, two frozen pizzas, a jug of ice tea, and a box of dog biscuits.

The Gimellis never question what you buy. It's like a code with them; they cash you out on the personals of your life, but never comment on how you live it.

"Eighteen dollars and eighty-two cents."

I slip Mom's twenty from my pocket, uncrumple it a little, and lay it on the scuffed counter. Mrs. Gimelli's hands are practiced and sure; she takes my money with one and counts out change with the other.

I'm standing at the door positioning my canvas shoulder bags (one reads: SUPPORT YOUR LIBRARY! TAKE A BOOK TO LUNCH in embarrassing, bright red letters) when Mr. Gimelli appears at my side. In one hand he's holding a dingy green watering can, water slopping over its rim. In the other hand is something wrapped in aluminum foil.

"You a good girl, been coming here for a long time," Mr. Gimelli says. "Take this as a gift for your doggy friend, okay?"

His smile is earnest, and I can't refuse. I blush and add the aluminum foil thing to my baggage.

"Thanks, Mr. Gimelli," I say, a little surprised. "What is it?"

"It's the bone marrow. All the dogs, they like that."

The whole walk home, I think about Diego. I wonder what part of his body he shot. I imagine Mrs. Nettlemoyer or some other teacher going to use the bathroom and finding Diego sprawled back over the toilet, blood sprayed everywhere.

Teachers are a peculiar breed. If there's a most forgotten culture in the world of high school, it's teachers. Who survives high school and wants to come back later?

The kitchen counter is littered with empty soda cans and bank statements. I use one of my shoulder bags to swipe clean a place to set it down. The stove clock says 4:18. Two hours before Mom gets home.

Ordinarily, I'd take my walk in the woods now. But I blew off letting Mrs. Menapace's dog out in the morning. The dog is probably pissing all over the floor by now.

The dog.

The dog needs a name. I put the bone marrow and dog biscuits into a less cumbersome backpack.

Big Girl. Horse. Bertha.

I recite names in my head all the way to Mrs. Menapace's. I could just ask Mom what her real name is. Mrs. Menapace probably told her, or Mom could always go and ask her. But I'm hesitant. Mom might start asking me questions about the dog, the house, the responsibility, and I think it's probably best not to bring it up. Then I think about that stupid romance book I just finished, and a character who has been scorned by her lover. Fiona. In the book, Fiona is strong and beautiful, but easily deceived.

Fiona seems to fit well enough.

This time, I walk more easily up the steps to Mrs. Menapace's empty house. I feel less like an intruder.

"Fiona," I call out as I open the back door. The giant dog is waiting for me in the kitchen, her eyes doleful, her dish empty.

"Sorry, girl."

I fill the dog dish and give her a bowl of water. Fiona plunges her muzzle into the food, utters a massive burp when it's gone, and heads for the back door.

This time I don't ready myself to slam the door behind her when she comes back in. I watch her crouch in the back lawn, sniff a few random spots in the grass, then trot toward the back porch.

I still haven't touched Fiona, and I sudddenly want to pet her brown ears and that odd spot on the top of her head.

Before she gets to the porch, I take Mr. Gimelli's bone marrow from my backpack.

Fiona's ears perk at the rustle of aluminum foil, and she bounds up the three steps to my side. Her head is the size of our microwave.

I can't decide if I'm scared or exhilarated. My hand quivers a little as I extend the bone marrow toward her powerful jaws.

"Fiona, good girl."

Her face is intent on the marrow. Her intelligent eyes are a rich brown. She stands as high as my waist, lanky and muscular. She has huge whiskers, some black, some white, depending on the color of the fur from which they sprout. Her jowls are great drooping folds of skin and pink gums and drool.

"Here, Fiona, take it," I encourage her.

Fiona opens her jaws and I can see sharp white teeth, bigger than my own. But she takes the marrow from my hand so gently, I barely notice it's gone until she drops her haunches to the porch floor, the marrow in her mouth.

I wait until she's done. It only takes her a few minutes to crush Mr. Gimelli's gift and I watch her with awe the whole time.

After a few licks of her slobbery tongue against foaming jowls, she stands and shakes herself.

Now is the time to pet her.

I timidly offer my palm to her nostrils. Fiona seems uninterested and patient. I place my hand on that brown spot on her forehead. Her fur is short and wiry.

I run my hands over her for a long time. It's more amazement than affection, but Fiona seems content. After a while, I feel at ease with this dog that has to weigh a hundred pounds more than me. Not confident, but at least not about to lock her up and never come back.

Mrs. Menapace has a roll of paper towels above her kitchen sink. I clean up the three puddles and two craps I find in her parlor, then decide I like Fiona enough to try to scrub the pale brown stain that has formed at the edge of the carpet. Fiona sits beside me as I clean, no apology in her expression.

"I like you." I gently tousle her ears. My own voice surprises me. It sounds happy, and I wonder why, since I'm scrubbing dog crap.

I feel bad leaving Fiona alone. I decide she needs at least a couple of hours of my companionship on Saturday.

Since I have nothing else to do.

9 "Mom, I need to see the eleven o'clock news."

Mom is curled up on the couch in her blue bathrobe. There's no light in our living room except for the TV's flicker. She sits up, surprised to see me.

"What for?" Her voice is suspicious.

"Someone said one of our teachers shot himself. Maybe it'll be on the news."

Mom reveals the TV remote from within her billowy bathrobe sleeve and clicks to the local news.

"Why the hell would he shoot himself?"

I stay silent. Mom sounds bewildered and accusatory at the same time, like she thinks that somehow I have something to do with it.

"Eleven at eleven," says the anchorwoman. "Eleven nonstop minutes of news."

Mom grunts, like maybe she thinks that's not so clever.

Then there's a shot of my high school, the squat brown building.

I go numb, because now I know it's not just school bus gossip. It might actually be real. Mom gasps as the anchorwoman launches into a news story about an unidentified teacher taking his life in the teachers' lounge. Unidentified, pending notification of his next of kin.

"Christ almighty!" Mom bellows.

Grief counselors will be on hand. Self-inflicted gunshot

wound. No explanation for the suicide at this time. No note, that's all she wrote. Bye-bye, Diego. Curtains closed.

"Holy crap," I breathe.

"You knew about this?" Mom turns angrily to face me. "You knew and didn't think you should mention it to me?"

I feel my face burn, like maybe I did know something back at a time when I could have done something about it. Like maybe just one of us homeroom students could have given a damn and taken the matter of Diego's behavior this morning to the principal. Isn't that the principal's job, to make sure teachers don't blow their heads off in the teachers' lounge?

Mom is still ranting. Was he a lunatic? He had a gun in school? Didn't we hear about kids shooting their teacher every other week? He was a teacher, a *teacher.*

"My taxes at work," Mom says, concluding her litany. "We buy that guy a house and a car and whole summers off from work. How does he pay us back? Blows his head off in front of our kids."

I don't mention that it didn't happen in front of kids. I don't mention that nobody seemed to hear or see anything, not even an ambulance pull up at the school. We were probably all caught up in who has bad hair and who is fat and who is making out in the study cubicles.

Final Act—Teacher Kills Self in School.

I lie in bed that night and think first about Diego, then about Victor. Fat Boy, my closest thing to a friend.

Victor's family was friendly with the Shop and Run Gimellis. Italians are like that in our town; however welcoming they are to other cultures, they hold their own in the highest regard, its membership like an elite club. When Victor and I rode our bikes to Gimelli's for candy, Mrs. Gimelli would slip two extra Pixy Stix in our bag and wait patiently while we counted pennies, even the time we brought eighty-nine of them to her counter in a plastic Ziploc bag from Victor's kitchen drawer. We were kids. We had no idea it might annoy her, and she never let us think it did.

Mr. and Mrs. Gimelli always greeted Victor by name, but they never stopped calling me Victor's Shy Friend. Even one day when Victor explained to them that my name was Andrea, Mr. Gimelli nodded and replied, "Good boy, Victor, you and your Shy Friend come back real soon, and tell your momma we have spicy sausage fresh."

I ate dinner at the Rizzos' a few times. Mr. Rizzo pronounced my name "Onndrea." I had only been friends with Victor for a few months, but already Mr. Rizzo gave me little chores. *"Help set the table. Go find the big sauce spoon, not this little junk spoon that belongs in the rubbish bin. That reminds me, Victor, you and Onndrea drag the rubbish barrels out to the street after dinner."*

Not only was Victor overweight, he had a weird divot in his chin like someone had set a pencil there when he was a baby and the chin just grew around it until someone thought to take the pencil out, leaving a crater behind. Mr. and Mrs. Rizzo were pleased he had made a friend in his new neighborhood, as if friends weren't something Victor had come by easily before they moved here. I think about how hard friends can be to come by, and how so many kids resort to being friends with whoever is willing to have them. Could Ashley-with-Bad-Haircut genuinely *like* Teena Santucci? Or were the Cheerleaders friends with each other just because they'd been cast that way? Because over time, other kids forced them to collect in a group from which there was no graceful escape until high school ended?

There were others like me, too, the kind without friends. The kids who could blend easily into the woodwork. We learned to carry our faces blandly, to avert our eyes from everybody. We sit in unassuming places and get unspectacular grades. We want to get out of childhood with at least a little dignity intact.

I fall asleep thinking about Fiona. And wondering what Mrs. Menapace is like.

10 Saturday morning.

I used to spend Saturday morning watching cartoons and eating Pop-Tarts on the couch. It was the only day of the week I carried my pillow downstairs. I would prop it against the rough arms of the couch and lie under the quilt for a couple of hours, listening to more industrious neighbors mow their lawns. Mom slept late on Saturdays, then shuffled around in slippers and her bathrobe half the day before taking a shower.

Now that I'm older, I usually read in bed until Mom yells *Are you going to sleep all day?*

Today I'm up early, dressed in a pair of sweatpants and a baseball cap. There's no sound coming from Mom's room. I hold the screen door with my hand to prevent it from slamming as I leave; even the neighbors are just starting to stir.

Fiona is at the door. This time I caress her ears. Her tail wags, so I rub her chest next. She is still a towering monster of a dog, but I'm becoming more sure she's a civilized monster.

Already Fiona's feeding and trot to the backyard are getting to be a routine. She gently accepts a dog biscuit at the top step, and I stroke her muscular back.

I wander in the gardens for a while. Fiona walks beside me, never squashing a hopeful sprout of plant. She snuffles her nose in decaying leaves. She stands, nostrils flaring into the wind for a scent my own nose is far too weak to detect. She is beautiful.

One of the most extraordinary things about dogs is their total lack of self-consciousness. A dog never questions its own beauty, its own worth. A dog just accepts itself and lives for the moment.

After a while, Fiona pads up the back steps and stands at the door. She looks back at me with impatience.

"Coming," I say. I open the door for her and she trots inside, toenails clicking on wood, toward her water bowl in the kitchen.

I haven't yet explored Mrs. Menapace's house. Not that I haven't wondered about it. But I'm too afraid the pleasure will be ruined by guilt. What would I say if Mrs. Menapace walked in on me while I was checking out her bedroom?

But I decided today I might glance at Mrs. Menapace's painting easel. Hanging around so Fiona had company means I need something to do. The parlor has no TV. It would have looked out of place there anyway.

Fiona returns from the kitchen and presses against my side, forcing my hand to rest on top of her head. I scratch it a little and notice a writing desk I haven't seen before. The desk is tucked in a corner next to a ceiling-high bookcase. It's overflowing with papers and books. Pencils are jutting at all angles from a cobalt-blue ceramic jar.

The sheet of paper on the makeshift clothesline next to the easel has begun to pucker from hanging too long. I wonder if I should take it down for Mrs. Menapace. I move closer to see it.

The carpet muffles my jittery footsteps. I'm half expecting Mrs. Menapace to step through the back door with a hospital bracelet still dangling from her wrist. *I've been released, and just what do you think you're doing, snooping around?*

I step around a coffee table to get the proper angle to see the painting. It's a painting of a garden scene in early spring. Snow-stunned shoots and black earth. Each individual sprout looks almost hopeful. Ivy, entangled in an ornate bench, looks suddenly liquid after a winter of brittle death. The sky looks chilly and distant, the sun not as close as a midsummer sun.

In the lower right-hand corner, there is a marking in black paint. On closer inspection, I make it out. *H. Menapace.*

Helen? Helga?

For a while, I explore Mrs. Menapace's parlor, avoiding places I think could be too personal: drawers, cabinets, and the mail basket on top of the desk. I don't want to be a total snoop. Fiona is passive about my intrusions. She stays close as I study the titles of the books on Mrs. Menapace's shelves. *Human Anatomy for the Artist. An Illustrated World History. Selected Works by Elizabeth Barrett Browning.*

The papers covering the desk are scraps, the handwriting difficult to read. Some of the notes appear to be peculiar reminders:

Which insects come out first, and what do they really look like?
Plant morning glories.
Notice sun just before noon.
Brush Zena, leave fur for birds.

Zena.

"Zena," I say. The dog's ears perk. She seems to hesitate for a moment, like she's expecting a command to follow her name. When no command comes, she just thumps her tail on the carpet amiably.

The easel is positioned in a corner of the parlor where sunlight seeps around a gauzy curtain. Its backside is to me, and when I look around to its front, I'm disappointed to find it empty. I wonder where more of Mrs. Menapace's paintings are kept. An old hermit artist must have stashed away plenty of them over the years. I find more paintings stacked in stiff cardboard next to the fireplace, beneath a heavy black velvet drape.

I decide not to look at them, at least not now. Unbundling them was a more serious breach of privacy than just wandering around the parlor.

I let Zena outside one more time. Before I head home, I put a handful of dog biscuits in her damp mouth.

"Be a good girl, Zena," I say. "See you tonight."

11 Monday morning at school.

There are six television news vans parked in the front parking lot. Parents are gathering at the auditorium entrance. Principal Guthrie is dressed in a dark suit, standing near the flagpole and nodding vigorously at a TV camera.

Mom drives me to school, which she has never done before. Like it's some sort of motherly duty to deliver me to the unfolding drama of my school, postsuicide. She complains that she can't find a parking space while I survey the crowds in front of the building. A few kids are acting like it's any other normal day, but most are taking in the scene with faint concern or bewilderment. I see a Channel 68 reporter approach Wendy Cartwright with an extended microphone. The Doughnut is right there. She steers Wendy away as if the reporter were a child molester. Once she has Wendy out of harm's way, she turns back to the reporter and waits for her to try to approach another kid. The Doughnut looks fierce.

"This is bull crap," Mom mutters, and I wonder if she means the lack of convenient parking spots or the postsuicide drama playing out in front of my school.

Mom marches up the sidewalk toward the auditorium, and I'm afraid for Principal Guthrie's safety.

"Go to your homeroom," she instructs me, and I hurry away from her before someone figures out she's my mom. She acts as though Diego's death is a personal matter between her and the school district, even though she's never met a single one of my teachers. How can she be so angry at everybody? It makes me tired just to think about her dedication to it.

The first bell rings. The Doughnut, Fag Feet Ferris, and a whole army of teachers are guiding students into the building. It's the regular routine, they say, over and over. Go to your homeroom.

Ashley-with-Bad-Haircut slams her locker just as I open mine. She looks at me, and I resist the urge to look back. Nonetheless, she speaks to me.

"This is some crazy place, huh?" she says.

I nod. Then I figure it's worth a little more than that. She didn't need to speak to me at all. There was nothing in it for her. And yet she did it anyway.

I turn to Ashley, whose hair looks a little less severe today.

"I have homeroom with Diego," I say. "Had."

I instantly feel stupid. Ashley doesn't seem to notice just how stupid I am. She shakes her head in empathy.

"That's going to be pretty weird."

I nod again, and Ashley offers a wan smile and disappears down the hall.

"Good luck," she says as she passes.

Pretty weird, yes.

———

43

Homeroom is silent, except for the creak of elderly chairs beneath fidgeting kids. At first, no adult shows up, and kids start looking at each other, alarmed. Have we been abandoned? I start to feel as if we deserve it somehow. Kids who normally look right through me today meet my eyes, guilt and shame reflected there.

The nerd who sits next to me flicks my elbow and mouths something at me I can't understand. The football players look glum; one cracks his knuckles until Nicole shoots him a glare.

"Sorry," he whispers, then coughs.

The second bell rings. I'm sweating.

Then, thankfully, there are footsteps in the hallway, and Fag Feet Ferris enters the room. With him is a lady I've never seen before. She's wearing a polyester blazer with a VISITOR name tag on the lapel.

Mr. Ferris doesn't say anything. He looks around the room, his eyes shiny. Then Val Amman starts bawling.

I cringe in my seat. The nerd next to me is frantically trying to get me to look at him, but I refuse to acknowledge him. I stare at the places where the polyurethane on the surface of my desk has been worn away by countless propped elbows. Out of the corner of my eye, I see Mr. Ferris approach Val and place a hand on her shoulder.

Val wails harder. Mr. Ferris whispers something, and Val stands up noisily. Mr. Ferris guides her into the hallway.

"Ladies and gentlemen, my name is Mrs. Hillary," the lady who came with Ferris says. "District psychologist."

"Many of your parents are in the auditorium having a meeting about our crisis." Mrs. Hillary begins walking down an aisle on the other side of the classroom. "They are worried about you.

"The best thing you can do to get through this, and make some sense of it, is to talk about it. So, talk."

We all remain mute.

In the hallway, we can hear the constant tone of Mr. Ferris's voice and the hiccupy weeping of Val Amman.

I want to be anywhere on the planet but here—in the former homeroom of Mr. Diego.

Mrs. Hillary nods as if she's expected our silence. She allows us to keep it for several moments more before she launches into a speech on grief, healing, and accepting what we cannot change.

The nerd, who has become impatient, suddenly leans over and slides a newspaper clipping between my elbows.

EDUARDO P. DIEGO

Eduardo P. Diego, 48, of 567 Winterhaven Apartments, died Friday as the result of a gunshot wound.

Mr. Diego was a teacher at Simmonsville Public High School for 17 years, where he also served as curriculum advisor. He was a former Debate Team coach, Chess Club mentor, and Kayak Club leader. He is survived by his mother, Francesca Y. Diego of Patriotsville, Ohio; a sister, Helena C. of Waterville, Ohio, and several nieces and nephews. His father, George E., died in 1995.

Born in Patriotsville, Ohio, Mr. Diego

was a graduate of Ohio State University, where he earned a master's degree in education. He was a communicant of Our Lady of Solace Roman Catholic Church, Simmonsville, where he served as a lector and prayer group leader.

There will be no calling hours or service. Burial will be in Patriotsville Cemetery, Ohio. Contributions may be made to the Simmonsville Ambulance Corps, P.O. Box 33, Simmonsville, PA 13111.

I read the obituary three times. I think about the tie slipping through Diego's fingers to the floor of our classroom, his soft words, "That's it, ladies and gentlemen." That's it. Show's over.

My head is pounding. I recite over and over in my mind, *That's it. That's it. That's it.* I cannot hear Mrs. Hillary. I don't want to hear Mrs. Hillary.

With a shaky hand, I pass the newspaper clipping back to the nerd.

If you close your emotions off so the bad stuff can't get in, you make it so the good stuff can't get in either, Mrs. Hillary is saying. Val is still whimpering softly in the hall.

That's it. That's it. That's it.

Mom's car is in our driveway when the bus drops me off.

I stand at the curb in mild shock, staring at the car and willing it *not* to be there. I stay there until Mom opens the front door and hollers, "Andrea! I'm home!" like I don't already know that, and I'm not standing there thinking I might be able to just run down the street and hide at Mrs. Menapace's for a couple of hours.

But it's too late for escape. She's looming there with her fist propped on her hip, her face expectant. Then Gloria's head is in the doorway, too, and I am defeated.

I trudge across the lawn to our front steps. To Mom and Gloria.

"The school recommended parents be home to meet our kids after school today," Mom says by way of explanation. "We're supposed to make sure you're doing okay, considering your teacher blew his head off."

Gloria steps aside to let me enter my house. She's wearing the same hospital cafeteria uniform Mom wears every day. There are sensible shoes on her feet and a hairnet on the back of her head.

Gloria looks at me like I have a dead rat duct-taped to my face.

"You look a little white, honey." Gloria puts her clammy

hand to my forehead. "This ordeal must be making you sick, how could it not be making you sick? It's making me sick, sick to death."

Mom snorts at her. The silence that follows makes Gloria uncomfortable.

"Come on in, honey," she says finally.

There are two wineglasses on the coffee table.

Gloria is saying how she worked the six-to-two shift today and came right over seeing how we might need a little help around the house, considering all that's happened.

"Sit on the couch, Andrea," Mom says. "You're okay. Right." She says it like it's an order, not a question.

Gloria flutters behind me, making a drama of getting me a pillow and quilt. Mom walks over and takes a big swig from her wineglass, draining it.

I say nothing.

"The school gave us some pamphlets and papers and stuff," Mom says. "Something you might want to read."

She drops a handful of brochures in my lap. I look at the top one. *Helping Your Child Cope with Trauma.*

"Give me a break," I mutter. Mom has never been one for finesse.

Gloria disappears into our kitchen and returns with a wine bottle. She fills Mom's glass, then tops off her own.

"You know, what Andrea needs is something to calm her nerves," Gloria says to Mom. I see her wink at the wine bottle.

Mom grunts. "Andrea, drink a glass of wine and rest awhile," she instructs.

"You know, European kids start drinking wine when

they're like six years old." Gloria chatters while she bustles back to the kitchen for a third wineglass. "There's nothing weird at all about a little kid asking his parents for a glass of wine down there in Europe."

Mom smiles at Gloria, shaking her head. "It's *over there* in Europe. Not *down there*. *Down there* is South America. Europe is *over there*."

Gloria starts giggling to cover the fact that my mom can ruin any moment.

She hands the new wineglass to Mom. Mom fills it halfway and hands it to me.

The wine is red and bitter. Gloria tells me to hold the wineglass by the stem part, not the cup part.

"Then you stick out your little pinky, like this." Mom takes the cue and is giggling with Gloria—or at her.

I drink the wine in one long gulp. It tastes bad, but I like the warm sensation that runs from my throat down to my fingertips and toes. I feel my neck relax a little.

"Now just rest awhile," Mom directs, taking my glass away.

She and Gloria ignore me, having done their duty. Mom is showing Gloria the old CDs stacked inside the cupboard, groups like Van Morrison and Steppenwolf.

I doze off.

13 Dad didn't come home sometimes.

I don't think he meant to be disrespectful to Mom and heartless to me. He was just that kind of guy. And he drank too much, too often. When he made it home after a day or two, there would be crazy fights in the kitchen. Mom telling him to pack up his stuff and get out. Dad telling Mom to lighten up, since when was *she* perfect? She drank, too.

But to Mom, there was a difference. Mom could have a few drinks and still be Mom. Dad, on the other hand, forgot his own name.

Finally, Dad disappeared for a full week. No phone call, no nothing.

Mom stacked Dad's things in a corner of the garage and got a restraining order against him. He gave her a divorce and custody without a fight. One week. It changed our lives, our personalities forever, that week. At least it did for me and Mom. Dad's probably out there, pretty much the same. But I hope he noticed that a certain daughter of his was no longer part of his life.

Maybe he thought I was better off.

14 It's midnight.

I can make out Zena's massive shoulders in the moonlit kitchen. She's like a statue except for one giveaway—her tail is tapping on the kitchen floor.

"I'm so sorry, girl," I say.

For a moment I have no idea where the lights are in Mrs. Menapace's kitchen. I run my hand along the wall just inside the doorway. Nothing.

Then I remember the string hanging from the ceiling. I fan my arms wildly in the air until I feel the string against my hand. I grasp it and give a sharp tug.

"Oh, Zena," I say. "Poor girl."

I woke up fifteen minutes ago, still curled up on our couch, in a dark house. Gloria gone. Mom in her own bed, snoring softly.

I immediately thought of Zena.

It feels cruel to leave a dog alone for so long, especially a dog like Zena. We carry out our new but comfortable routine of food, water, and a visit to the backyard.

From Mrs. Menapace's back porch, I can hear the melody of spring peepers. This is one of my favorite sounds of spring. The symphony of frogs comes from everywhere in the marshy part of the woods. They are a million tiny violinists warming up their instruments, each with its own style. There are deep baritones and willowy sopranos, some chirrups more boisterous, others more pensive. All unaware of me and my giant companion listening to their tribal song.

It's a beautiful night. The stark lines of the garden by daylight are soft now. I can see the shape of lilac trees by the subtle changes in black hue. There's no breeze. Zena licks her jowls, then lies next to me on the porch. It's nice to just sit and listen.

I like to touch Zena's ears. When I was small, I had a soft yellow blanket. Its edges were satin, and I'd lie in my bed and rub the satin between my fingertips until I got sleepy. Rubbing Zena's ears reminds me of that blanket.

"Zena girl," I whisper in the ear my head has come to rest on. "Let's go for a walk."

Zena's head tenses.

I use a tiny laser-light key-chain flashlight to find my way to the garden shed. Mom gave it to me in my Christmas stocking last year.

"It's a tool no latchkey kid should be without," Mom said that Christmas morning. She stayed wrapped in her heavy bathrobe on the sofa all that day, reading the romance novel I had given her, *The Litany of Lisa*. Third in a series featuring Lisa and her sultry life.

Kneeling beside the Christmas tree, I had used the key-chain flashlight to make a miniature laser-light show on the bare living room wall. Then I latched it to my key chain just in case I needed to thwart a rapist at Gimelli's Shop and Run with my dazzling light show.

Tonight, though, the flashlight has finally come in handy.

In the half-moonlight, I can easily make my way to the ivy-shrouded garden shed in Mrs. Menapace's backyard.

The shed is not a typical garden shed. While everyone else on our road has the same aluminum box, white with blue trim, Mrs. Menapace's shed is built of thick stone. The stones are not rough-edged, but smooth like giant pebbles. In the daylight, the stones are different shades of brown and washed-out gray. From its roof to the ground, lush green ivy grows like a waterfall. Once, when I came to let Zena out, there was a wind that ruffled the ivy leaves and made it look like ripples in lake water. Tonight the ivy is motionless and inviting.

The door looks like a large wood barrel, flattened. There is a wrought-iron latch for a doorknob. I train my laser light on it and wonder if I should go in. Zena positions herself beneath my palm, nudging me for a pat.

I expect the garden shed door to creak when I open it, but it swings open smoothly.

"Just need to find you a rope leash, girl," I whisper to Zena. She gives me her doleful Saint Bernard look, ever-patiently waiting for me to hurry up and get on with it already. I step inside the pitch-black shed.

For an anxious moment I wait for a bat to flutter against my face or a mouse to scurry out of my path. It's not that I'm ordinarily afraid of bats and mice, but in this unknown dark terrain, I know it would spook me to meet wildlife.

Zena's toenails click on the shed's floorboards. After a moment my eyes adjust and I realize that the moon is barely glowing through the shed's window. Just enough so that the contents of the garden shed begin to take gloomy shape.

My flashlight beam reveals a utility-sized flashlight, hanging from a piece of twine on a nail under the window-sill. I decide to risk the neighbors' attentiveness and use the bigger flashlight. Even if Wendy Cartwright's parents no-ticed a flashlight beam from Mrs. Menapace's back garden shed, would they do anything about it? Would they react the way we all did in Mr. Diego's homeroom the morning he shot himself? I remove the shed flashlight and turn it on. A sudden blast of light fills the small space.

The flashlight reveals a workbench, painted white and lightly stained with soil. A stool. Shelves of cans and bot-tles: house paint, window cleaner, wasp bombs. Highest up, glass bottles labeled in Mrs. Menapace's scrawly hand-writing: *Renaissance Lavender. Opal Pink. Autumn Bonfire Orange.*

Then there are more shelves, these holding neat rows of chalky white pottery. Bowls and vases, urns and platters.

Zena snorts and shakes her head.

"Well, if you're impatient, tell me where to find you a leash," I scold her, but my voice is gentle. Zena wags her tail.

A few steps away is a pottery wheel. It's the kind where you kick the bottom with your foot while you hunch over a spinning tabletop. There are streaks of dried clay on the surface of the wheel in perfect concentric circles.

There's a tray of tools next to the pottery wheel, things that look like thin chisels at the orthodontist's office. I notice one that's a strip of metal between two wooden handles. There's a wooden salad bowl holding a sponge, half submerged in murky clay water.

In the other corner of the shed is a stainless steel box about the size of a TV set. There are dials on its top. A pottery kiln like the one in the corner of the art room at school. This one is much smaller.

Large iron tongs hang from a hefty hook just above the kiln. There are shards of broken pottery swept neatly into the corner, a broom propped alongside. Dried plants are suspended upside down from the ceiling; there's a pair of clay-crusted canvas overalls hanging from the back of the door.

Zena lies down, watching me.

I play the flashlight past one particular shelf, just above the kiln. There are several pieces of pottery on it. At one end are two bowls, painted in pale, lifeless hues. I gingerly touch one. The surface is brittle and coarse; the paint seems to have been absorbed too deeply.

At the other end of the shelf there are more bowls. Each has a sheen of rich color on its surface. I pick up one bowl and carefully set it on top of the kiln for a closer look.

I'm amazed at how thin the bowl's walls are, because it feels so sturdy. Inside the bowl is turquoise, like the water of some Caribbean bay I have only imagined. Outside, it's pocked with chocolate brown and midnight black, swirled together. In the flashlight beam, it looks like a glass marble was melted over the surface of the bowl.

I set the bowl back on the shelf with anxious hands and

survey the shed again. I find a coil of rope on the floor next to a strange, short metal barrel encased in what looks like chicken wire.

"Ready to walk, Zena girl?"

Zena, who has lain expectantly on the floor as I browsed her mistress's shed, thumps her tail. When she stands and shakes, I laugh.

"You sound like a horse clomping around in here," I say.

Zena wears a rolled leather collar, too thin to hold her back if she really wanted to get away. It's more like a necklace than a collar. I hesitate. Then I figure that, collar or no collar, if she really wanted to get somewhere, all it would take would be a powerful jolt to yank my arms out of their sockets. I could be known around school as the Girl Who Broke Both Her Arms While Taking Care of Some Old Lady's Pet. I picture my own mummified arms extended on metal rods for six weeks.

Though she's a short-haired Saint Bernard, the wiry fur on the back of Zena's neck half hides the collar. I find a metal hoop in the collar near her throat and firmly knot the rope there.

"Let's do it, girl."

Zena pauses when I hesitate on the garden path. She doesn't sit down. Her nose quivers. The peepers are still filling the woods with their shrieks.

During one of my previous visits, I noticed a gate in the fence at the far end of Mrs. Menapace's property. Zena trots toward the gate as if she's known we were going there the whole time. I consider how badly Mom would lash out at me for walking a stranger's dog in the woods after midnight, not telling a soul where I am. But who is there to tell? Who would understand?

This gate creaks when I swing it open. At first I don't see the beaten-earth pathway between scruffy bushes, but Zena knows it's there. She guides me until I'm more sure of my footing and pace. We're headed for the part of the woods I like best.

Night-walking in the woods is exhilarating. I clutch the flashlight in one hand and Zena's leash in the other. Zena doesn't pull, only stops occasionally to inspect an ordinary rock or stick. I let her sniff, and in the moments of silence while her nose twitches and I'm motionless, I can feel the liveliness of the woods at night. Unseen small creatures scurry away from Zena and me. A deer crashes through some bramble off the path, but I'm not afraid. I can hear my breath entering my lungs. I breathe in unison with my own footsteps because the rhythm of it feels right.

That night in my bed, I wonder about myself. Me, Andrea Anderson. I know I'm plainish and boring. I know that my teeth are crooked and my nose is passable. I'm not a good student and I don't make anyone smile just by entering a classroom. But could there be something about me that could interest other people? It almost seems like a wild fantasy.

15 At Gimelli's Shop and Run, Mr. Gimelli has a package of free bone marrow waiting.

"Your dog, she like it?" he asks, his eagerness like a little kid's.

"She loves it," I answer, my cheeks burning. "I should pay you for it."

Mr. Gimelli waves his hand in my face, as if he's insulted. I shrug sheepishly.

It's a pretty hot day for May, and as I trudge home beneath the weight of four Lean Cuisines (*Buy three, get one free!*) and canned fruit, I feel the sweat beading on my body. Roger Dupris and his friends are out in the Duprises' driveway. Roger is casually holding the basketball under his elbow. His face widens into a smile when he sees me, looking like a camel laden with market goods, at the end of his driveway.

"Andrea, are you going tomorrow?"

I gasp, then cover it with an awkward cough.

Roger's friends turn and look at me doubtfully. Roger seems unaware that he is stretching the social seam by calling out to me, Andrea Anderson.

"Don't know," I mumble.

"*What?*"

Roger's friend Keiran Fleet rolls his eyes at my timid fumbling.

58

"Don't know."

Roger allows the basketball to fall and bounce on the asphalt a few times, then decides to walk a little closer to me. I feel my heart beat faster. *Am I about to be made fun of?*

"I figure as many of us that can go ought to go, out of respect and all," Roger says.

Diego's family hadn't wanted a funeral. After some pressure, the school decided to let the student council organize a memorial service in the auditorium Wednesday night. Seven p.m., bring your tears of self-pity and leave them on the movie-theater seats.

The truth is, I want to go to the memorial, but I don't want to sit alone. And I don't want Mom to come along and start asking the other teachers if they bring guns near our precious kids.

So I've basically decided I'm not going.

Roger's friends back off from their scowling and start playing basketball again. I look at my sneakers.

"Well," says Roger, who doesn't seem the slightest bit uncomfortable. "You should come. You were in his homeroom and all."

"Maybe," I answer. Roger smiles at me again before returning to his game.

Ladies and gentlemen, *that's it.*

ACT

2

Thankfully, I'm in an appropriate place when it happens.

It's eight in the morning, and Zena and I are in the kitchen. The dog food is clattering into Zena's metal bowl when I hear the back door thump closed.

I freeze.

A thief? Mom coming to finally check up on me with this whole dog thing?

Then there's a commotion as Zena changes gears from placid dog to ecstatic puppy. Her toenails clatter as she runs, in a way I haven't seen Zena run, down the hallway to the back door.

"Zena, baby!" a voice greets the Saint Bernard rocketing to the back door. "Come here, my baby!"

I still don't move. I feel like I've snuck into the boys' locker room to use the bathroom after school because the girls' is being cleaned. Just in time for the football team to walk in from practice. My pants around my ankles. I feel like I might pee right there on Mrs. Menapace's kitchen floor.

Zena reveals my presence to Mrs. Menapace by prancing joyfully into the kitchen. I hear a bag drop to the floor by the doorway; then there's Mrs. Menapace in the kitchen doorway and there's me, clutching Zena's food bowl as if I've been caught clutching a bottle of brandy from her liquor cabinet.

Mrs. Menapace is tall and thin. She is wearing a sweater that is way too warm for the weather and a pair of baggy hospital pants.

Her face shows no surprise.

"Check this out," she says to me.

She extends her left foot toward me, and the too-long pants move up a bit to reveal a bony white ankle.

"Cardboard slippers. I wore cardboard slippers down Webster Street to call a cab. Wore them home in the cab.

"The best part is I asked the cabdriver to stop so I could buy a Three Musketeers." Her foot flops back to the linoleum, but her eyes never leave mine. "I walked down the aisle of the gas station minimart, and my feet sounded like I put Kleenex boxes on them."

Mrs. Menapace laughs so I can see her back teeth.

Mrs. Menapace isn't old. She's maybe a little older than Mom. She has long brown hair with a few streaks of gray. It looks like it hasn't been combed for a while, and I think of Ashley-with-Bad-Haircut.

But Mrs. Menapace's disheveled appearance is appealing. She's pretty. Her face is pale, but her eyes are gray and mischievous.

Zena nuzzles her mistress. I feel a moment of jealousy, followed by shame.

I'm still mute.

Mrs. Menapace comes toward me, her cardboard feet shuffling on the kitchen linoleum.

"Let me get a look at you."

I shrink away from her outstretched hands, but she pretends not to notice. Then her palms are on my cheeks and

64

she holds my head steady. Her face is close, and I smell cheap soap.

My face turns beet red, but Mrs. Menapace is serious. She looks me in the eye, and I want to struggle free and run.

For some reason, I don't.

Mrs. Menapace's retreat is as sudden as her advance. She backs away and moves to the kitchen sink, where she takes a kettle from a hook above her head and begins to fill it with tap water. Zena remembers her hunger and clomps to my side. She nudges the bowl with her snout, snapping me out of my statue routine.

I decide to go ahead and feed her while Mrs. Menapace busies herself spooning herbs from a canister into a metal container the size and shape of a Ping-Pong ball. Home-made herbal tea.

"Do you like your tea with milk?" Her back is to me. Zena's bowl clatters on the floor.

"I have to go to school now," I whisper.

"What grade?" Mrs. Menapace scuffs her cardboard slippers to the refrigerator.

"Tenth."

She nods and Zena belches.

"Come back after school, then," Mrs. Menapace says. "If you're not busy, that is. You've been so good to Zena, and I'm not sure I'm strong enough yet to take her for a walk. Could you do that?"

I feel a rush of relief. Zena isn't going to be taken away from me.

At least, not yet.

2　Diego's homeroom is a little more normal.

Not much more, but at least the football players aren't wide-eyed and nervous, and Val Amman isn't bawling. The nerd who sits next to me whispers that he heard that Mr. Ferris is going to take over our homeroom permanently, and did I know he was arrested once for sitting in a tree in California because some mall developer was going to cut it down?

"I didn't know," I say. The nerd smiles his wide, grateful smile.

"Some three-hundred-year-old sequoia tree or something like that," he says, proud to be the Minister of Information. "He was a protester and he sat in the tree for like a week to prevent Tree Murder."

I think about Mr. Ferris sitting in a tree for a week while I watch Nicole scrutinize her face in a tiny mirrored compact. The nerd is still whispering to me when Mr. Ferris walks in, blinking in his usual confused way and glancing at his wristwatch.

When Mr. Ferris does roll call, he uses our first names. It sounds strange to me, like he's shaken up the fundamental order of our homeroom and made it random. As though we've become different people, a whole new cast of characters. I listen carefully as he calls out each name, until he gets to the nerd who sits next to me.

Jeremy.

Other than homeroom I have no classes with Jeremy this year, but last year I listened to him get verbally abused in Spanish class.

Jeremy is gawky, brainy, and outspoken. It's that last quality that makes him a mark; the kid has just never learned to keep his mouth shut and lie low.

Germy, are you gay?

He would get asked this with such regularity I began to think he was gay just because I associated him with the obnoxious question. Every time he conjugated a verb for Mrs. Esposito, every time he raised his hand or answered a question, his abusers would lick their lips and whisper, *Germy, are you gay?*

Jeremy bore the ridicule. It didn't help that he always sat so primly at his desk. Some boys mimicked his way of sitting, crossing their legs tightly. It was hard not to make fun of Jeremy. Not only was he just uncool in every way, it was almost like he made a point of being uncool.

In homeroom, though, no one has made fun of him this year. In fact, no one has made a venomous remark to me this year, either. I keep tabs on this, and assume the day will come when I'll be singled out. I'll trip over a football player's splayed-open legs while walking to my seat, and get called a Skank. Someone will announce that my backpack smells like a dead cat.

But Jeremy doesn't seem to care one iota that he's a

target, chosen on a whim for the way he inhales or the shade of denim of his jeans. He's been there many times, and survived.

"Ladies and gentlemen." Mr. Ferris hops up onto Diego's desk and sits, swinging his feet like a little kid. "There won't be any more classroom visits from school psychologists, but they've set up a little gypsy camp in the main office if you want to go visit.

"You can just go down and make an appointment, and they'll give you a hall pass. Use them, guys. They're here to help. There's no shame in having a rap session with an adult when a teacher dies. It's hard, we're all taking it hard, and believe me, it helps."

First bell rings, but no one moves because Mr. Ferris hasn't finished.

"I've gone to see the counselors. I've talked it out. It doesn't make it go away, but it does make you sort it out in your own head, and a confused brain is a tough place to live."

Mr. Ferris nods. We all stand up like we're incredibly tired.

3 The Doughnut is wearing a black ribbon pinned to her dress, right on top of her mountainous left breast. She is standing in her doorway, surveying the stream of students that pass by without acknowledging her.

"Mr. Marcus, keep your hands to yourself," she commands one second. "Maxine, you dropped your pen," the next.

I hunker at my locker, digging for my biology lab notebook without much interest in whether or not I will actually find the stupid thing. I tear my thumbnail on my English journal, which was thrown on top of the whole mess anyway, and look up at the Doughnut in exasperation.

I want to tell her to shut up.

Normally, the Doughnut doesn't notice me. I'm not a kid who requires her admonishments and directives, so she pays me no mind. But today the Doughnut looks right at me. Her face looks surprised.

"Andrea, is there a problem?" She says it like she hopes there is indeed a problem, so she can issue some response from her well-rehearsed repertoire of responses.

I shake my head sternly.

The Doughnut keeps looking at me, her eyes searching my face. I glare at her. I want to find my damn biology lab notebook so I can slam my locker and leave the Doughnut in the dust.

"Are you sure you're okay, Andrea?"

I feel the muscles in my face change, and a surge of panic wells up in my throat, followed by hot bile. I'm either going to throw up or start crying like Val Amman. Neither choice sounds like something I want to be doing in front of the whole school. I'd be known as the Girl Who Puked in Her Locker.

Then big hot tears spurt from my eyes and the Doughnut is there, sweeping me into her classroom with a meaty arm.

"I'm fine," I hiccup. "I just can't find my notebook. You know my name."

The Doughnut nods and guides me into the walk-in storage area at the back of her earth science lab. It's gloomy and smells like dust.

"Away from prying eyes," Mrs. Donough explains, propping me against a worktable and uprooting a crumpled tissue from her pocket. Her face is filling with genuine concern, and I cry harder. She just stands next to me, her hand on my elbow, and lets me cry. She doesn't appear uncomfortable, and I'm thankful for that.

"Mr. Diego's death will affect us all in different ways. Sometimes the effect will come at inopportune times," she says. "I cried all the way home driving on the expressway yesterday."

I feel instantly guilty.

I'm not crying about Diego. I'm crying because she knew my name, back there in the hall when I wanted to scream at her for being annoying.

I don't feel anything about Diego.

I cry harder.

"We all feel a sense of loss." Mrs. Donough digs a pad of hall passes and a pen from the pocket of her dress. "Time will heal us all. Summer vacation is just around the corner." She scrawls a message on a hall pass.

"What's your next class, honey?"

"Biology lab. Mr. Ferris."

She adds Mr. Ferris's name to the hall pass.

"I gave you an extra five minutes on here, Andrea, so you can stop by the girls' room and wash your face," Mrs. Donough says kindly. When she gives me the hall pass I notice her hand is so fat, it looks like her knuckles are indented.

"Thanks."

It's all I can say without crying again.

The hallways are empty. Teachers' voices drone behind closed doors. I feel like a mouse.

I decide the hell with my lab notebook. I go into the girls' bathroom three doors down from Ferris's class. The last stall door is always closed, instead of half open like the others. Most girls avoid it because you never know if someone is in there. It's just not worth the embarrassment of shoving the door open on someone, or bending over with your backside to the sky to see if there are any feet sticking out. Plus, some girls are kind of particular about you staring at their feet while they use the toilet. Sharon Newkirk might just punch you in the nose should she find you peering under her stall.

71

But today I know it's mine. No one's in the bathroom. The fluorescent lights are dimmer here in the last stall than in the others. The paint finish on the walls has been chipped away to form dull, metallic messages: *Yvette is a bitch* near the toilet paper dispenser. A short distance away near the tampon disposal: *Randy is a dog.* A little arrow pointing to these two unrelated carvings fueled by adolescent hatred: *They should have puppies.*

A poem in black ink above the door handle:

> *I was here*
> *But now I'm gone.*
> *I left my name to carry on*
> *Those who liked me*
> *Liked me well.*
> *Those who didn't*
> *Can Go to Hell.*
> *Sondra*

I've never carved a message on a bathroom wall. I've never sat in a bathroom stall long enough to experience literary inspiration of toilet-sized proportions. But today I find the angst of these girls who had sat there somehow soothing. Their desire to be alone, yet speak out at the same time. For some reason, this calms my nerves. I work a pen free from the spine of my English notebook and press it to the stall wall. It takes quite a bit of pressure to get the ink to stick to the slippery wall, which makes it seem like more of a commitment to deface the bathroom.

EPD
RIP

I write it in thick letters. It means:

Eduardo P. Diego
Rest in Peace.

I study my message for a long time. It seems pretty strange to write something like this on a bathroom wall. It seems pretty strange to cringe every time someone looks my way. It's definitely strange to have an imaginary dog you call on your walks in the woods, then leech onto the dogs of neighbors for companionship.

Strange is so arbitrary, yet so vital to a person's existence. What made me suddenly strange, or was I strange from the beginning and just not yet aware?

The bell rings a short time later and the bathroom door almost immediately swings open. Three goody girls planning a movie and a sleepover. I flush the toilet and leave the stall, wondering why it feels like high school will never end.

Mom is home when the bus drops me off.

Again.

This time, she's not handing me wine and bereavement pamphlets. She's playing an ancient Blue Oyster Cult record and applying makeup at the bathroom vanity.

"Andrea, I've got a date," she says. There's a hint of excitement in her ordinarily deadpan voice. "It's this guy at work.

"I've had lunch with him twice, just in the hospital cafeteria." She wrinkles her nose as she puts on lipstick. "But today he asked me to dinner and a baseball game."

Mom hasn't worn makeup in years. The last time I saw it on her face was at my grandma's funeral, when she got drunk in her parents' kitchen and we left in a hurry. Her lack of experience in the makeup department shows.

I stand in the bathroom doorway and watch my mother. She's not entirely bad-looking when she smiles. Her hair's brown and limp like mine, but hers is cut short. Her face is round and she has an extra chin. Her stomach sticks out suddenly below her rib cage.

For her date, she's wearing baggy jean shorts and a white blouse, tucked in. Her legs aren't bad, but then there're these ugly manlike sandals on her swollen feet.

"How do I look?" she says. Her eyes are hopeful. I crack a small smile back.

"Rub in the cheeks a little more. You look nice."

"I don't know what I'll do for the next hour," Mom complains. "Maybe I'll straighten up the living room just in case he comes inside."

Mom hurries past me to fluff pillows and fold the quilt.

"I need to go let out Mrs. Menapace's dog."

Mom nods.

"I'm sure Mrs. Menapace will be out of the hospital soon. Surprised they've kept her this long." Mom is almost chatty.

"What's wrong with her?" I ask.

"Oh, just a hysterectomy. I guess she started hemorrhaging at home, that's why she called the ambulance. But then they just take out your ovaries and uterus and it's pretty routine from there."

5 Roger Dupris's driveway is empty. It's too hot for basketball.

I hesitate at Mrs. Menapace's front door, wondering if I should knock, now that she's home. Finally I decide to round the house and go through the back gate. Zena greets me as the gate swings wide, and I can see Mrs. Menapace near her pottery shed.

The heat of the last few days has transformed the gardens. Timid shoots have found strength in the sun and are unfurling themselves. The greens are more vibrant. The haphazard tulip bed, colorful just a few days ago, has already passed its prime and begun to dull.

"Mrs. Menapace?"

Mrs. Menapace doesn't move. She's sitting with her legs crossed in the dirt, her palms upturned on her knees. The bulky sweater and hospital pants have been replaced with a gauzy sundress that looks like it might have been handmade somewhere like Nepal or Thailand.

"Mrs. Menapace?"

After a moment, Mrs. Menapace turns her head to me as though she's heard me the whole time. She smiles and adjusts herself back into the position I found her in, face tilted to the hot sun.

I approach a little closer, but not too close. Zena

sniffs a patch of soil left in a mound next to the herb garden.

I'm not certain what to do.

"Honora."

"Pardon me?" I say.

"Call me Honora. Mrs. Menapace was my mother-in-law. I'm Honora."

Mrs. Menapace exhales and, catlike, hops to her feet. Her exotic dress twists up a bit to show pale legs.

Honora is pronounced Ah-*nora*.

"Did kids make fun of you when you were in school?" I am horrified at myself for asking.

Honora considers the question.

"For my name? No," she says. My face is burning with shame, but Honora seems unaware of my discomfort. "For other things? Yes."

Honora walks along the garden path. Despite looking so ill, she moves with self-confidence. She gives me a pleasant smile.

Zena trots over to her.

"Some tea?" Honora asks. It's too hot for tea, but I nod because I don't really know how to say no to tea twice in one day. I don't think I've ever drunk a cup of tea in my life.

Honora drifts to the porch. On the top step, there's a glass pitcher filled with brown liquid. Floating on its surface is something that looks like seaweed, and clots of dirt. Honora lifts the pitcher to the sunlight and narrows one eye at it.

"Looks done," she says. "Maybe a bit on the young side."

Then she disappears into the house. I pat Zena's head while wondering if I'm meant to follow her. Then the porch door swings wide and there's Honora holding two glasses of ice and what looks like a spaghetti strainer.

Honora doesn't speak while she strains out the muck at the top of the pitcher and guides the brown liquid into our glasses. I study her. She's showered since this morning. Her long hair is tied back in a scarf that doesn't match her dress. She has no makeup on. There's a pendant around her neck—a yellowish-brown stone surrounded by silver filigree. Cat's-eye.

Her feet are bare and her toenails unpolished. When she raises her ankle to absently scratch it, I see huge calluses on the sole of her foot—the type people get from walking around barefoot all the time. There's a silver ring with a hint of turquoise encircling the toe next to her big toe.

"Yarrow, nettles, and a hint of chamomile," she says, taking a long swallow while I hesitate. "Yarrow and nettles are good for a woman's reproductive system. Chamomile disguises their bitterness."

I nod, as if it were a perfectly routine thing for me to suck back a glass of reproductive-system-enhancing herbs. Then I taste it. It tastes like dirt and dead leaves and tree bark.

Honora smiles and reaches out to touch my cheek. I shrink away, wondering why she always wants to touch me. We sit side by side on the bottom porch step, looking out over the gardens. Zena's bulk is blocking much of the view.

"Do you have any kids?" I ask, fighting the urge to ask for a glass of water to rinse my mouth.

"One," Honora responds. "A son. He's grown and lives in New York. Not the city. Actually it's about as far from the city as you can get. The Adirondack Mountains."

I nod, pleased that I was capable of starting a normal conversation. Then I find myself speaking again and not liking the words coming out of my mouth.

"How come no one ever sees you?" I say. "I mean, no one in the neighborhood knows anything about you. I thought you were really old."

Honora throws her head back and laughs. I shudder with embarrassment. Her teeth are straight and white, and I wonder how they've stayed so white if all she drinks is mud.

"I guess I'm a bit of a hermit," she says, still smiling. "But I'm a hermit who genuinely likes people. Or likes genuine people, I guess you'd say. I'm busy, and I like my own company. I find what goes on in my head quite fascinating, and I like my own friendship best. How lucky is that?

"And you, too, Zena." She rubs a skinny forefinger around the edges of the perfect circle of brown on Zena's head.

"Tell me about you," Honora says.

I feel panic rising. Honora is so fascinating. What could I say about me that even remotely compares?

"Start with your name," Honora suggests, seeing my hesitation.

I think about the Doughnut suddenly. *Andrea, is there a problem?* Her voice so concerned. I feel a new wave of guilt washing over me.

"Andrea Anderson," I say.

Honora has turned to face me. Her eyes are looking

right into my own, and I feel like she can see right through me, like she already knows I'm plain and boring. I look at the porch railing, pretending to study the grains of unpainted wood. I feel my shoulders slump with the rejection I know is coming, the look of disappointment surely about to leap into Honora's eyes, releasing plain and boring Andrea Anderson from her interest and allowing her to slop back into the murky category of Unimportant.

"A very strong name," Honora says, draining her tea glass. "One that suggests a continuation of experience."

"Oh. What do you mean?"

Honora stretches her legs and splays them out on Zena's back, working her toes into the dog's fur.

"You have the word *and* in your name twice. And And. I believe that's a hint that there's always something more to come, right? I believe that there's an endless depth to you, but it may not be apparent at first. You are not a surface person, are you, Andrea Anderson. You are continuing."

I don't know what to say. Television advertisements pop into my head: *And that's not all! You'll also get six replacement filters for your vacuum cleaner if you act now! And that's not all! The first five hundred callers will get this handy car vacuum. And wait, there's more! A free bottle of carpet cleaner . . .*

"I'm not sure you're right," I say.

"I'm sure I'm not wrong." Honora smiles. The whole conversation has me bewildered.

"Do you want me to walk Zena for you?"

Honora stands and brushes off the rear of her dress.

"Yes. And I'd be pleased to pay you for the fine job you've done caring for her this past week."

I've hoped to avoid the whole act of payment for my services. Not only do I not know what my time was worth, but paying me also seems, well, final. Like that's it, paid in full. Done and over.

I'm not ready to lose Zena yet.

Zena, having picked out the word *walk* from our conversation, begins doing a little dance of joy at our feet. I wonder how Honora knows I've walked her before. I never had permission to do anything besides feed her and let her out to pee.

"How do you know I've done a great job?" I ask.

"Because dogs never lie," Honora answers.

"I can't accept any money," I say. "I liked it. I like Zena. She's a friend."

I wait for Honora's eyes to fill with pity. I wait for her expression to register the picture of Andrea Anderson: Pathetic Friendless Nothing.

It doesn't happen.

"Zena's good like that," she says. "You can walk her whenever you want. It's not like it would break her heart to get walked more often." Honora moves toward a rosebush that has caught her attention. I watch her lift a limp stem, her fingers gentle as though lifting the wing of an injured bird.

6 I decide to attend Diego's memorial.

It's funny how something as simple as an interesting conversation and walking a dog can give you courage. Honora would go, if she were in my shoes. Or would she? Well, either way, she wouldn't let the excuse of sitting alone in the auditorium prevent her from going. She *prefers* sitting alone. I've never known anyone who preferred sitting alone. It's liberating to think I have that option.

Mom is gone for her date when I get home from Honora's house; there are two empty wineglasses on the coffee table.

It's still unbearably hot, so I put on clean shorts. I wonder if this is disrespectful, wearing shorts to a memorial service. But I have to ride my bike, so wearing a skirt is out. Pants—the thought is too horrible. So it's shorts.

It's nearly seven o'clock when I coast into the school parking lot. Six miles feels like twelve in this heat. I'm surprised to see television news vans parked in front. When will *that* end?

The auditorium is packed. There are huge ancient fans blowing hot air on the crowd, which comprises whole families: moms and dads, little kids, most dressed casually. Teena Santucci and Ashley-with-Bad-Haircut slide into the back row with me. They leave an empty seat between me

82

and them. Teena ignores me; Ashley offers a quick, wan smile. Then two more Cheerleaders appear and Teena flaps her hand at me. She's dismissing me before she's even acknowledged me.

"Scoot down, we need two seats."

I scoot. I decide that if my face burns red, people will just think I'm hot in this crowded, poorly ventilated auditorium. I gaze around the place. Roger Dupris is in a white shirt and tie, sitting with his mom. A group of football players is milling by the doors, folding their arms across their chests and refusing to sit down even though the skinny senior class president is using his best manners while asking them to do so. Fag Feet Ferris and his pixie wife are there. So is the Doughnut, sitting by herself and clearly listening in on a discussion taking place in the row in front of her among some Goth boys.

Fag Feet and the Doughnut have way too much job pride. It's like they live here or something.

Then the curtain opens like we're at some sort of play. Four people appear, three students and the music teacher Mrs. Whittaker. They're poised with musical instruments, sitting very erect on folding chairs in front of shiny metal music stands.

The students have two regular violins, and one of those huge violins that sits on the floor. Mrs. Whittaker is wearing a white blouse with great sweeping sleeves; her arms are cocked at either side of a big gold harp.

"Oh, for crap's sake," one of the Cheerleaders mutters. "Wake me up when the fa-la-la is over."

Softly, Mrs. Whittaker counts *one-two-three*, and the

quartet begins. It's a melancholy song, but the musicians' faces are emotionless.

The National Honor Society gets up and files out of the front two rows of the audience. They walk onstage, each kid carrying a lit candle. The candles are inserted in a series of plastic-looking candleholders on the floor behind the musicians. While Principal Guthrie greets the restless crowd, I see Mr. Ferris working his way down the side aisle toward the stage. Mr. Ferris—always in the middle of everything. He waits while the National Honor Society kids make their way down the steps, then climbs the steps himself. He appears weary. I note he's wearing corduroy pants and a corduroy blazer in this heat. Apparently, Teena Santucci notices, too.

"For chrissake, look at Fag Feet Ferris in corduroy. You can see sweat stains in his pits, how nasty," she hisses to her friends, who giggle in acknowledgment of her superiority on the subject.

"I heard his wife doesn't shave her pits," Ashley-with-Bad-Haircut offers. "Or her legs, either."

"Now, *that* is nasty," Teena responds.

Mr. Ferris nods at Principal Guthrie and clears his throat a few times. He grins a stagestruck, foolish grin at the audience, then seems to remember the purpose of this whole ceremony and abruptly becomes solemn. He waits for Principal Guthrie to exit, stage left, before he speaks.

"Ladies and gentlemen." His voice sounds apologetic in the microphone. "Boys and girls. Friends."

He allows this last word to impact the restless crowd.

Few take notice, but at least the Cheerleaders have put their running commentary on hold.

"Each candle you see here onstage represents a year of service Mr. Diego gave to our school." Mr. Ferris sweeps his arm wide to encompass the display of candles. The armpit of his brown blazer is dark, and Teena Santucci shudders. I feel beads of sweat forming along my nose and wonder what will happen if the Cheerleaders notice me engaged in the crass act of sweating.

"Eduardo Diego was a good teacher, and a good man," Mr. Ferris is saying. "He was a friend of mine. He gave his *all* to the school community. And nothing can erase that, nothing can take that away from us, all of us who benefited from his patience and dedication in so many ways."

The Cheerleader sitting next to me snorts.

"Yeah, did *I* ever benefit from that weirdo," she says. "Diego was an ass, everyone knows it. I mean, *Christ* already."

"It's freaking hot. Want to go to the mall after this?" Teena is admiring her fuchsia fingernails. "The stores'll be open for another hour or so."

"I don't think I will," Ashley says, as if going to the mall is too ordinary. Mr. Ferris has yielded the stage to an Honors English student, who's reading a poem. I wonder if she wrote it, or if it's Emily Dickinson or Robert Frost or someone. Muffled laughter erupts from the football players standing at the back of the auditorium. Teena Santucci cranes her neck around to see the source of hilarity.

"Oh God," she whispers to Ashley. "Mitch Halligan keeps trying to rub some Dork's ass."

"What?"

Ashley-with-Bad-Haircut and the two other Cheer-leaders turn to see. I can't help myself and glance over my shoulder too. There's big Mediocre Football Player Mitch, snickering with two other guys. Seeing the Cheerleaders glance, Mitch sneaks his hand behind a guy whose face I can't see and gooses him.

The Goosed Guy moves away a few inches. I can see now it's Nerd Jeremy. His eyes are locked on the poetry-reading Honors kid, but there's a twitch at the edge of his mouth.

Honors kid leaves the stage to a spattering of applause. Some man wearing a gray polo shirt gets up there next, introduces himself as Reverend Frye from the Simmonsville United Methodist Church, and makes a big deal about how the prayer he's about to lead is nondenominational. After the prayer, he says, there will be a Moment of Silence.

"Isn't there something like a law about how you can't talk about religion in public schools?" one of the Cheer-leaders whispers. "Principal Guthrie should get his balls busted for this."

A mom escorts a wailing toddler out of the auditorium. The microphone hums. There's coughing and rustling. Then the quartet strikes up again, and the memorial service is over. Everyone rushes to exit the auditorium. Off to the mall, or to ice cream stands. Relieved.

I run into Roger Dupris and his mom in the lobby, trying to make my escape.

"Hey, Andrea." To my horror Roger is making his way toward me through the crowd. "My mom is letting a bunch of people come over to my house for a swim in the pool. It's so hot. Want to come?"

I cringe visibly, but Roger just smiles and shrugs as if it doesn't matter to him either way. Then his mom appears and makes a fuss over how I've grown and why doesn't she see me around the neighborhood more?

"Come over, Andrea," she pleads. "It was hot enough in that auditorium to fry a chicken, and you kids deserve a little bit of kid time."

Roger blushes.

I ponder for a moment the Embarrassing Mom Factor. Almost every mom has this personality trait. Without even realizing their own uncoolness, moms say things or act in a way that is a humiliation for their teen children. I wonder if Teena Santucci's mom ever burst in on her friends and offered cookies and Kool-Aid, announcing "It's chock-full of vitamin C!"

Probably.

"No thanks, Mrs. Dupris," I mumble. I'm certain Mrs. Dupris has put Roger up to this, told him he could only invite friends over if he invited that poor Andrea Anderson Girl Who Has No Friends. Charity case. Mrs. Dupris was known for organizing canned food drives for the hungry of Simmonsville.

Oddly, Roger looks disappointed instead of relieved.

"Well, if you change your mind, you know where we live," he says.

Outside, a steady stream of cars is trying to make a left turn onto County Route 11. I stop my bike at the end of the school's drive and wait for a break in traffic. Sweat is already making my eyes burn.

"I can fit your bike in the back if you want a ride."

Ashley-with-Bad-Haircut is driving her parents' minivan.

She can't possibly be talking to me. I look behind me to see if there's another kid on a bike. Maybe Bryan Davenport's sports car is in the shop.

Ashley laughs at me, but not unkindly.

"Come on," she says. "It's air-conditioned."

"No thanks," I mumble, but Ashley is already pulling out of the line of traffic onto the shoulder of the road. I consider racing away on my bike before she can even get the car in park. Then the hatchback pops open and Ashley is striding toward the back of the van.

"My dad always takes the backseats out for the dogs," she explains. She grabs the handlebars of my bike and starts lifting it in.

I help, because there's nothing else to do at this point. A car slows next to us; two Desirable boys whistle out the window.

"Like those muscles, Ashley," one says. They continue when the car behind them honks.

"What-*ever*," Ashley mutters. I wonder if she is embarrassed to be seen with me, if she will be questioned later by her friends. *What were you doing with that weird, ugly girl?*

Inside the car, the air-conditioning is wonderful on my face.

"I only got my driver's license last week," she says, smoothing her gray eyeliner in the rearview mirror with a pinky finger. "So if you want to run screaming from the vehicle, now's the time."

I laugh, even relax a little. Ashley drives cautiously. She reminds herself aloud to use the turn signal when merging back onto busy Route 11. Once we're on the road, she keeps her hands on the wheel and doesn't look at me.

"So where do you live?"

Little discoveries. Like when you find out a magnificent dog lives right down the road from you. Like when you find your grouchy mother at the bathroom mirror, primping for a date. Like finding out Ashley-with-Bad-Haircut, a girl entrenched in the cheerleading dynasty, a girl who has boyfriends and went to cool parties, might actually be a nice person. Even more amazing, she might actually be nice to *me*.

I tell her where I live. Then Ashley starts talking about how weird this whole Diego thing has made her feel.

"I don't like to think about death," she says. "My brother died two years ago. Since then, I think about death every freaking day."

There's no anger in her voice. Only hurt and wonder.

"How old was he, your brother?" I don't know what else to say.

"Twenty." Ashley rounds the turn onto my road. "Diagnosed with an inoperable brain tumor at nineteen."

I vaguely remember the guy. Not who he was, but the news stories, a plaque on the gymnasium wall. Track and field star.

"So now I'm an only child." Ashley follows my pointing finger into my driveway. "But my brother's ghost still lives

89

in my house. Right on my parents' faces. Probably on mine, too. His death permanently blew our minds."

Ashley turns to look at me for the first time. I study her face. Gray eyeliner, a wan smile.

"I'm not so great at backing this barge out of driveways," she says, starting to laugh. "Mine has this big ditch at the bottom. First time I rode a bike, I cruised down it, flipped over the handlebars, and landed in the ditch. Now every time I back this thing out of my driveway, I think about that."

"Thanks for the ride," I say, feeling about as socially inept as I ever have in my entire life. "I turned sixteen two months ago, but my mother probably won't let me drive until I'm forty."

Ashley laughs, and we both get out into the blazing heat. She helps me extract my bike from the coils of rope and electrical cords stowed in the back of the minivan.

"My dad's a contractor," she explains. "Does house renovations and stuff." She wipes at my handlebars with the hem of her T-shirt. "You'll probably find black dog fur clinging to your bike for a week."

"What kind of dog?"

"Dogs. Three. Two are black Labs, the third is my dad's pride and joy—a Newfoundland. That's like a black Lab, only way bigger and way hairier. Drools like crazy, but he's a pretty great dog."

"I love dogs," I say. I tell her about Zena.

"So you know about drool," Ashley says. "I've got to run. If my mom knows the memorial service is over and

I'm not back, she'll think I'm drag-racing her dorky mini-van on the interstate or something."

I wave to Ashley, who hesitates four or five times before she manages to back out of our driveway. Then she honks a farewell, and she's gone.

My house is still empty. Even though it's only a little after eight o'clock, I climb into bed with a book and blast the window fan on high.

All in all, a pretty amazing day.

The next morning, I allow myself to let my guard down. Just slightly.

Mom leaves for work before I wake up; the fan's burring noise has drowned out any evidence that she came home at all. But her bed looks disheveled on one side, so I figure she came home at some point. I'm grateful it hasn't played out like one of her TV sitcoms: Mom Home from Date Sits on Edge of Daughter's Bed and Tells All. Too corny.

But I feel like today just might add up to something. I allow myself an extra minute at the bathroom mirror, just to study my own face. My nose is passable, that's about it. For me, it isn't going to be about looks.

Instead it's time for me to stop wallowing in the confusing lie, the one about how all girls turn out pretty. That's what little girls believe, and our society doesn't teach plain, ugly girls who hide in the shadows how to survive. I've been waiting for a lesson, but it isn't going to come.

If all things were fair and logical, I would walk down the hallway of Simmonsville High School this morning to a warm greeting from Ashley, a disappointed smile and *"Where were you?"* from Roger Dupris. The Doughnut would comment to me on the hot weather.

I allow myself the fantasy for about two minutes. But nothing in the halls of Simmonsville High School has changed. Ashley is too deep in conversation with Teena Santucci to notice me at my locker. Roger Dupris isn't anywhere to be found. Even the Doughnut is busy, barking out orders over the chaos of homeroom-bound kids.

Making Out Couple sits next to me in the library carrels again. This time I spend forty minutes tracing the indents of graffiti on the desktop. Thinking about Victor Rizzo.

The problem had been Victor's older sister, Maria. She got caught up in a wild crowd in Simmonsville, which I guess is not an impossibility. Snuck out all the time, got a reputation for hanging out in the cemetery with any breed of freak who handed her a pill. This was noticed by Victor's parents with no small amount of anxiety. Then Victor's mother was rifling through Maria's purse and found Ecstasy. Tiny, hard pills that landed Maria in rehab.

Maria stayed a few weeks; then a few weeks later Mr. Rizzo got a new job in his company. Then the family moved Maria and Victor to Akron so Maria could have a "fresh start."

Italian families do what it takes to take care of their own, Mom had explained to me as I sobbed on my pillow the day the moving van cleared out the Rizzos' house.

"Stop crying about it," Mom said. "People do that. They leave."

They had lasted in Simmonsville just eight months.

Some friends cling to each other for a while when one moves away. They vow never to forget each other, never to lose track of the details of each other's lives. Victor and I basically shook hands at the bottom of my driveway. That was it.

8 After school, I walk to Mrs. Menapace's house. Zena greets me at the back gate with her usual enthusiasm. Mrs. Menapace is bent over one of the diamond-shaped herb beds. She's holding a spade and studying a handful of seeds. There are small green plants in sod boxes strewn around her, garden tools, and a can of water.

I clear my throat and she smiles without looking up.

"Henbane. Poppy. Hops. Yarrow. White dead nettles."

"Huh?"

"Isn't it fitting?" She looks up at me. Her face looks much healthier today, as if a week at home in her gardens has warmed her. She looks younger, and I wonder how old she really is. Forty-five? Thirty-eight? Maybe she's younger than Mom after all.

"It really is," she continues, although I have no clue what she's talking about. "I'm planting the ancient herbs that were used to heal women's reproductive ailments. Right at the feet of my Naked Man statue!"

I laugh, unexpectedly.

"I swear, I didn't consciously plan it that way, Andrea." She chuckles. "Do you know that in medieval times, people thought that if you ate a flower the color of blood, you could stop bleeding? I studied medieval history at Dartmouth. Women who hemorrhaged in childbirth were

94

given partridgeberries. That's it. Now they rip out your insides, and oh by the way, find cancer while they're at it.

"I have to go back to the hospital, Andrea, this time in Philadelphia. Can you watch Zena for me for the next few days?"

When I get home from Mrs. Menapace's, Mom is tearing open a Lean Cuisine.

"Where were you?" She's got that accusing tone, like I've been out trying to feed dog crap to little kids for fun.

I don't answer her.

She doesn't ask again.

"Aren't you going to ask me about my date?" she asks, her face sullen.

"Mom, how was your date?"

She half-smiles. Too cautious to grant the date a full smile.

"He's coming to dinner here Friday."

"Should I buy an extra TV dinner at the Shop and Run Friday?" I ask.

"I'll take care of shopping Friday," Mom answers, heading for the couch. "You just show up to dinner, okay? And curl your hair, or something."

The heat wave has subsided to a tolerable temperature. I gather my bedsheets into a cocoon around my body, starting at my feet and tucking the sheets around them tightly. I work my way up to my shoulders and head, then allow only my mouth to escape my mummification.

That school psychologist who came in the morning after Diego shot himself, No-Wrinkles Lady in a Blue

Blazer. She said something like if you don't let the bad stuff in, you don't let the good stuff in either.

Was any good stuff worth the anguish? I barely knew Mrs. Menapace, or Ashley, or Diego. All touched by so much pain. Ashley a survivor, Diego a victim. Which would Mrs. Menapace turn out to be?

I stare at my alarm clock.

ACT

3

1 In the daytime, Zena moves through the woods without grace. She's animated by the scents and freedom; she's careless and sometimes stumbles on mossy stones in the creekbed.

For her, a walk in the woods is joy. Watching her makes me wish I could draw, or use a camera properly. Her nostrils are flaring as she stands chest-deep in the creek, water rushing around her peculiar markings. She is breathtaking. Her liquid brown eyes are both wild and soulful. She's not less intelligent than a human; she possesses a different kind of intelligence altogether.

It's Friday afternoon, and Mrs. Menapace is in Philadelphia getting her first radiation treatment. Or chemotherapy. Maybe they're the same thing. Zena is mine, but I feel no pleasure. Mrs. Menapace is really sick.

Mom is poring over a cookbook when I get home. It's the one Mrs. Rizzo gave me from her own kitchen a few days before she moved away from Simmonsville.

"You don't need to be Italian to cook Italian, even though most mamas think so." She winked at me. "You make yourself nice dinners, Andrea. Use this to make the prosciutto tortellini you like so much."

Mom has the cookbook flipped open to some pasta plate with sprigs of parsley and alfredo sauce.

"Damn, I forgot to get more butter," she says. "Oh, wait, it's still in the grocery bag."

Mom is wearing elastic-waist black slacks, the kind you see ads for in the newspaper coupon sections: *Extra-wide waistband for your comfort! One hundred percent polyester for easy wash and wear!*

Her hair is combed nicely, though, and she's wearing makeup again.

"Hey, Mom, rub in the cheeks a little," I advise.

Dennis shows up at six-thirty.

I argue with Mom in the kitchen when she tells me to go answer the door.

"He's your date, Mom, you answer the door!" I hiss.

"For chrissake, Andrea," Mom snarls.

Dennis doesn't ring the doorbell again, but taps gently to remind us he's there, just in case we're arguing about who has to answer. Finally, I stomp to the door and swing it wide.

My first impression of Dennis is Clydesdale horse.

"Oh, come in, Dennis!" Mom calls from the kitchen like she's just then realized he's arrived. There's a clatter in the kitchen, followed by the pop of a cork.

Dennis plods into our living room and looks around. I stand back and size him up.

Dennis has auburn hair that matches the masses of freckles on his cheeks and nose. His eyes are buggish and he's the lumpy kind of overweight. When he smiles, his teeth are a little bit crooked, but not too bad. His eyes dart around the room, but he doesn't look at me. In fact, even when he says hello to me, he doesn't look at me.

100

"I'm Dennis," he says, like there's the chance I've never heard his name before. "Andrea, right?"

"Yes."

The formalities over, Dennis plops down on our sofa and studies the TV remote control buttons. I sit across from him in our old recliner and study my fingernails. Through the window, I can see the little kids across the street shrieking with laughter as their dad sprays them with a garden hose.

"Been hot, huh," Dennis mumbles.

Before I can respond, Mom bustles in, all bright eyes and smiles, carrying a TV tray of Cheese Nips and sparkling wine.

"So you two have met. Good." Mom sets down the tray on the coffee table and straightens up.

"Andrea, go get the coasters," she says.

Coasters? For as many years as I can think back, Mom and I have set any old glass on the coffee table. Rings have been embedded in its surface for at least a decade. Probably a century.

I take the opportunity, however, to escape the room. Mom is smiling at Dennis. Dennis is taking a good, hard look at the cover of *Soap Opera Digest*. What a pair.

"They're in the junk drawer," Mom hollers after me. "Way in the back."

I take my time locating the coasters and sauntering back to the living room. Once I've arranged one each beneath Dennis's and Mom's wineglasses, I return to the recliner.

"So what do you do, I mean at the hospital?" I ask Dennis.

Mom answers for him. "Phlebotomist."

"Oh."

"That's someone who takes blood from patients and does the testing," Mom says gleefully. She swigs her wine, then swiftly checks her upper lip for a damp mustache. She smiles, pleased with her medical knowledge.

At that moment, I realize something.

Mom is happy. This can only mean that either Mom has a thing for bloody needles, or she really likes Dennis the Clydesdale.

Mom jumps up and swears about the pasta. She isn't wearing her slippers tonight; instead her gremlin feet are encased in pumps. Pumps. The kind they wore in the eighties, which is probably the last time this particular pair of pumps was freed from the depths of Mom's closet.

Dinner is quiet, almost serene. Except somewhere between the undercooked pasta and the paper towel napkins folded to appear like real dinner napkins, I change my attitude. It's not like I suddenly decide to like Dennis. I decide to just let my mother go, since I've never been able to make her happy, just *me*. She needs to find something more. To find happiness.

"So it's been all over the news some teacher killed himself at the high school." Dennis talks like a guy who's spent a lot of time drinking with the boys in the den, watching sports. I half expect him to blow his nose in the fake dinner napkin. Or to lean his chair back and undo the top button on his polyester slacks.

"Yeah," I answer, guardedly. "He was my homeroom teacher."

"You ask me, these teachers are spoiled rotten," Mom says, revving up for a rant. "Who wouldn't want their jobs? Babysit for like five hours a day, get all those holidays and vacations."

Dennis grunts noncommittally. It is a skill to grunt with indifference, and I like Dennis for it. Strangely, it seems to neutralize my mother's venom.

"A pretty fucked-up thing for you kids," Dennis says thoughtfully, wiping his whiskers.

"Dennis!" my mother chides, but not too forcefully. Dennis furrows his brow at her, then realizes.

"Oh, I get it. I shouldn't say 'fucked-up' around a sixteen-year-old." Dennis winks at me. "Maybe she's never heard such foul language before."

I smile at Dennis over my defrosted cheesecake.

An ordinary smile.

Dennis the Clydesdale grins back.

2 I end up at Gimelli's Shop and Run on Saturday morning.

Mr. Gimelli is busy serving the local Italian community, who apparently show up early on Saturday mornings to begin preparations for Sunday meals. I wonder, as I watch a woman point at breads and pastries, what it's like to be so haunted by tradition. Victor Rizzo's mother was known to stay up all night tending to finicky recipes for holiday dinners.

Mom had forgotten the basics when shopping for her culinary debut Friday. Namely, Pop-Tarts and orange juice. I had headed out of the house as soon as I saw Mom's bedroom door closed and Dennis's shoes still under the dining room table.

Mrs. Gimelli and a hook-nosed woman wearing thick glasses are debating the best way to put sour cream in a pastry.

In fact, the Gimellis are doing a brisk business, which seems strange. I realize I've never been in Gimelli's on a Saturday morning. How odd to have lived so near something and never known it had a completely different personality when you weren't there.

I'm choosing between Strawberry Frosted and Blueberry when there's a tap on my shoulder.

How such a big, cumbersome guy like him could have

approached without me realizing, I'll never know. But there is Dennis Clydesdale, grinning at me in Aisle Two.

"Why are you here?" I demand before I can suppress my surprise. After all, the Shop and Run belongs to me, not my mother's oversized boyfriend.

"Your mom figured you might be in here. We were driving by," Dennis says. "Why don't you forget the Tony the Tiger crap and come with us to the Pancake House this morning?"

My face is burning with embarrassment. Who might see me talking to Dennis Clydesdale and know he slept over at my house after only two dates with my mother? Or, worse: who might think he was my father?

"I have to walk the neighbor's dog," I squeak.

Dennis shrugs.

"So we'll drop you off in front of the neighbor's house after breakfast," he says. "Dogs can't tell time, far as I know."

"This one might be able to," I reply.

Dennis buys me the Pop-Tarts (strawberry *and* blueberry).

"For breakfast tomorrow," he tells me as I cower at Mrs. Gimelli's register. Mrs. Gimelli acts like she doesn't know me. Like it's all business and none of *her* business why the Shy Friend of Victor, who has never set foot in her store on a Saturday morning, might suddenly appear there with a huge, red-haired man who just happens to be buying her Pop-Tarts.

Outside the Shop and Run, Mom waves to me from inside Dennis's car and points to the backseat. I wonder for a moment why Dennis came inside the store to find me, not Mom. It had probably been his idea to involve me in this pancake outing. I wonder why Dennis would care.

I endure a short stack with a side of bacon.

I try not to look surprised when Mom and Dennis talk about an antique show.

Antique show?

Then Dennis belches like a foghorn and Mom stifles giddy laughter behind her fist.

I figure this must be love.

3 Zena is loping along the creek bank. Her haunches are taut, her ears and nose are alert. I notice that somehow, a dog's most developed senses can be *seen*. Ears and nose are suddenly able to snap into visible focus. I can see when Zena is using these senses, foreign to me, by the position of her nose and ears. Would that ever be said of a human?

The creek banks are too unstable and steep to sustain any real trees and plants. Zena and I both travel at an angle to keep our footing. I discover Zena can run full speed at an angle. I'm pleased when I make it down the embankment to the creek without landing on my backside.

Zena is in huntress mode, but I doubt she could ever actually catch anything. She's fast and strong, but a Saint Bernard pushing two hundred pounds is no match for a squirrel.

Soon she returns to my side, panting heavily from yet another fruitless chase. She lowers her frothy jowls to drink creek water.

"Zena girl," I whisper into her neck. "Who's a good girl?"

Zena snorts, and we climb the creek bank together. She waits while I use her back to steady myself.

Each time I enter Honora's yard through the fence gate, I notice the steady advance of spring. Now everything is alive. The grass is long enough to mow. Homely white berries have erupted from the strawberry plants clumped near the gate.

When I was in the second grade, my mother enrolled me in Bible summer camp for one week. I'm sure it was a week when she had no other source of day care, since that had been a regular problem before I was old enough to watch myself. Anyway, the Bible camp teacher was this middle-aged woman with really big sideburns. Mrs. Kineally. Every day, Mrs. Kineally wore a button on her blouse that said THIS IS THE DAY THE LORD HAS MADE. She showed us pictures of Adam and Eve, who looked like pampered movie stars, naked in the Garden of Eden. Their midsections were concealed by lavish plant leaves.

I think I remember that picture because I thought it was so strange that Adam and Eve were naked, strolling through a garden.

But I also remember the garden. Lush, perfectly formed plants and fruits. Not a single drooping limb on the apple tree, not one bug-bitten fern frond. Too perfect.

For some reason, Honora's garden reminds me of Mrs. Kinneally and her faith in that picture. Now I'm wiser. In the second grade, I learned that perfection is beautiful. I believed in the distinction between right and wrong, good and bad. I believed that all grown-ups knew the difference and could help me to learn it myself. But somewhere along the way I got confused. Because the reality is, there is no black and white. Right and wrong, that's really just one person's perception of how things should be. Not how they really are.

I spend the afternoon reading a leather-bound *Field Guide to Wild Plants in Northeast America*, loaned to me by Honora. The book is organized by plant shapes and colors, with little descriptions of where the plant might grow and what its properties are. Mayapple is one I recognize from my walks in the woods. Umbrella-shaped, with poisonous berries on its underside. Likes dampness and shadow. I try to memorize the names of all the plants I already recognize. Indian grass, wild senna, boneset. The names are like beautiful music. Then I memorize some plants that I don't think I've seen, but I'd like to: Venus's looking glass. Ragged robin. Wild columbine.

Zena surprises me at Honora's back gate in the evening. She wags her tail, and I wonder if somehow I forgot to put her in the house when I left this morning. Then I see Honora by the garden shed, wearing another silky, flowing dress and dragging a bale of hay along a garden path.

"Hey," I yell.

"Hey," Honora responds. She lets go of the twine she's using to pull the hay and wipes her forehead.

"I like your dress," I say.

"Sari. Traditional clothing of Indian women. This one is actually a wedding sari, but I figured what the heck, I'll wear it to drag hay around the backyard. Want some tea?"

"Only if it's straight-up chamomile on the rocks," I say. "I'm not too crazy about the other gacky-tasting stuff."

Honora laughs and heads for the back porch.

"Hey, I thought you'd be . . . sick," I call after her, instantly feeling rude. Honora turns and shrugs.

"Guess I might be, but they said it takes a day or so for

you to feel sick after a chemo treatment," she says. "There's a lot I want to get done before I'm resting my chin on the toilet seat."

Honora's tea is darker than mine. We sit on the back porch steps and admire Zena.

"School ends in less than three weeks," I say.

"Do you have final exams?"

"Yeah. But I'm not too worried about them."

Honora reaches down and straightens the turquoise toe ring. For the first time, I notice a pale gray tattoo on the inside of her ankle.

"What's that of?" I ask.

"Chinese water symbol." Honora lifts her ankle for closer inspection. The tattoo looks smudged and faded. It's about the size of my thumbprint and shaped like the profile of a single wave in the ocean.

"Symbol of life. Got it in college. Which reminds me." Honora allows the sari's hem to fall. "I'm going to need an assistant. You don't want pay for walking Zena, but this assistant thing is a paid position. The pay is bad, and the work itself is odd hours and odd tasks. If you're not interested, that's okay. But if you are, you're hired."

Zena walks over and snuffles our feet.

"What's an assistant do?"

Honora traces her finger around the perfect circle on Zena's forehead.

"I'm going to get a lot sicker before I get well," she says. "There's Zena, there's housework, there's food shopping, there's gardening. There's helping me get my pottery to different galleries.

"I'm thinking seventy dollars a week. Like I said, a couple hours in the morning, a couple in the evening, maybe some extra when I need to drive my pots to Barneveld or transplant my hosta plants. It's time to split some out and put them along the back fence line."

"I don't have my driver's license yet," I tell Honora. "I mean, if you ever wanted me to drive."

Honora shrugs.

"That's up to you," she says. "You can always get your learner's permit, if you want. Right?"

"Okay," I answer suddenly. "I'll take the job."

"Okay, then."

I don't want Honora to realize I'm bursting with happiness at her job offer. It's a sensation I rarely feel, but I don't dare savor it here in front of Honora.

"Can you start tonight?" Honora gives me a mischievous grin.

"Tonight?"

"Well, I'm fully expecting to start puking come tomorrow." There is no fear in Honora's voice, no dread. "So that only means one thing. Tonight, we raku."

4 I am amazed when I read Mom's note.

Gone bowling with D. Back late. ☺

Mom actually drew a smiley face. I chuckle at this bizarre behavior. Snaggletoothed Mom using a pen to draw a smiley face at the end of a note. I heat one of her Lean Cuisine dinners in the microwave. At least now I won't need any excuses for being out late, too.

From all my romance novel reading, I've learned a few things. For example, some women are happy only when they have a man. They have no self-esteem unless a man gives it to them on a daily basis. I consider the idea that my mom is one of these women. Maybe. I'll probably never know for sure why she operates the way she does.

Dad disappeared about the time I started school, and I've stretched my memory back as far as I can for times spent with the three of us as a family, doing something a family ought to do. I always come up empty. Just as I've imagined my own dog on my solitary walks in the woods, I've imagined trips to pick out my first bicycle beneath the smiles of my parents, Christmas mornings that sparkled with togetherness. But there had never been any of that. My mother's stern face and commanding tone dominate my memories; my father's bristly chin and gentle words are hazy moments conjured from a past so distant, it might as well be a dream.

I feel no pity for Mom, no disdain. Only sadness. I'm scared I may end up like her.

I go into the bathroom and frown at myself in the mirror. My face betrays my happiness over Honora's job offer. I realize it's probably betrayed me before—like in my surprise over Ashley's friendliness.

But it's still a plain face.

"Andrea," I say to the mirror.

It looks strange, to see my own detached mouth form a name I rarely say out loud. Hearing my name reminds me of rejection, and hope, and tears masked by long hair.

"It's time to accept the outside world for what it is. Time to explore the inside of your head for what's there, instead," I tell the mirror.

It sounds so simple.

5 Zena is tense.

"She hates fire," Honora explains. "She doesn't trust it."

Dusk has faded to dark in Honora's backyard. It's still warm. I hear the peepers in the woods and consider telling her about my first walk with Zena. Honora is busy arranging small piles of hay next to the ten or so metal buckets she has set behind her shed. The buckets are dented and coated with a skin of rust.

"This will be an intense couple of hours," Honora says, standing back to survey her work. The buckets and their corresponding hay piles are in a ring on the lawn. At the center of the ring is a stone platform, partially covered by the chicken-wire garbage-can contraption I've seen in her shed. There's a propane tank about the size of a small refrigerator nearby, with a tube and spray nozzle attached to its base.

"My personal rendition of Stonehenge," Honora says, bowing and waving her arm at the arrangement of buckets. "Oh, wait. We need the big tongs and a couple of lawn chairs."

Honora positions the lawn chairs a few feet from the chicken wire. I wonder if we're too close to the weird propane contraption. Honora is glowing like it's a treat to sit next to a flaming propane tank in one's backyard at night.

"Timing is everything when you raku pottery," she explains. "There's lots of ways to do it, but basically you fire your pottery. Hawaiians made pyres and buried pots in the smoking embers for days. In fact, every civilization that's used pottery has used fire. Nowadays we're spoiled by putting our pots in electric, controlled environments."

"Kilns?" I ask.

"Electric kilns. Which are great, but there's nothing like direct fire for pottery."

Honora hurries off to the pottery shed and returns with four pots hugged to her chest. She's wearing cutoff jeans and a sleeveless tunic. She told me to wear nothing "swingy" or "hangy" for this, my first job as assistant.

Honora's arms and legs are thin. Her ponytail's been anchored tightly into a bun at the back of her head. She instructs me to lift up the garbage can. I help her set the pots on the stone stage; then she adjusts the garbage can over it all.

"What's this thing called?" I ask.

"Raku kiln. Made it myself. Works pretty good."

Honora fires up the propane. It hisses, like our barbecue grill does, just before it ignites.

"Might as well take a chair," she says. "I'll give you your instructions while this batch heats up."

After we're seated, Honora aims the nozzle into a hole at the bottom of the raku kiln and pulls some sort of trigger. Blue propane-fueled flames illuminate the base of the kiln. Each piece of pottery inside begins to glow at its base.

"God," I breathe nervously.

"Hope your mother never said you couldn't play with

fire, because it gets even better," Honora says. The uneven spray of fire from the end of the nozzle makes eerie shadows play across her face. Zena is crouching nearby, watching the kiln. Her fur looks distorted: white parts glowing, dark parts missing.

The raku kiln looks like a garbage-can jack-o'-lantern. There is some kind of nonflammable insulation lining inside the chicken wire. Honora and I can see the pottery through gaping holes in its side, glowing red.

"Dante's Inferno," she says above the blasting gas noise of the propane tank. Water beads have formed on the surface of the canister.

"We have to keep the temperature constant for a while. When you see the sides of the pottery get a strange sheen, like the pots themselves are about to melt, we pull them."

I nod in agreement, like I know exactly what she's talking about.

"That's where you come in," Honora continues. "You are the Fire Master."

I feel a curl of excitement form in the pit of my stomach. Or is it fear?

Honora will place each piece of scorching-hot pottery on a pile of straw. I'll use a rake to cover the pottery with the straw. The straw will ignite in a ball of flame.

"You watch each piece until it's ready to be snuffed out, then drop a metal bucket over it." Honora's face is shiny with sweat from the kiln. "The lack of air will extinguish the fire.

"The secret is timing." Honora squats so close to the flaming raku kiln that I resist the urge to pull her away. "It's got to happen bam bam bam, or we'll miss the optimum moment."

"How will I know when to snuff out the flames?" My voice sounds shaky.

Honora shrugs. "Wait until you have consistent ignition, but no longer," she replies. "That means wait until the straw really catches on fire, count one-two-three slowly, then snuff it. Ready?"

I realize there's no fire extinguisher nearby. We've had so little rain. What if the grass catches fire and rages out of control?

"I don't think I can do this," I whisper, but Honora either doesn't hear me, or she ignores me.

"Here it comes!" she cries, and shuts down the propane canister. Then she whirls around with a huge oven mitt on her hand and sweeps the raku kiln up and away from the glowing pottery inside it. In the next moment, she is clutching a vase with long tongs and wasting no movements to get it to the first pile of straw.

Honora is all business and controlled urgency.

"Oh, God," I say.

The vase lands in the straw pile with a gentle thud, and Honora whirls away to get the next piece.

"Rake," she instructs over her shoulder.

I rake. I expect the fire to happen like a firecracker exploding in my face, but the glowing vase just smolders in its bed of hay for a moment. I have just enough time to back away before the straw bursts into a healthy crackle of fire. I'm mesmerized. Through the blazing straw, I can see the shape of the vase, withstanding the abuse of fire without damage.

"Snuff it!"

I grab the metal barrel next to the fire, feeling the hairs on my arms prickle with heat. I drop the can over the fire.

"Next one!" Honora is yelling. "Do a couple at once! Don't think too much!"

I have no idea if I'm performing my role as Fire Master correctly, but I'm sweaty and anxious from the pace of it. I glance at Honora's face to see if it's registering disapproval at my performance. I see rapture and determination. She's beautiful.

"One more!" she shouts.

Smoke is singeing my eyes, and my lips are dry from the fierce heat. Finally, the last pot is snuffed. I'm exhausted. I'm exhilarated.

"Ready for round two?" Honora asks.

"There's more?"

Honora disappears into her shed and returns with four more unfired pots. I make fresh piles of hay near the metal snuffing barrels, and we repeat the whole process from the beginning.

When it's all finished, Honora and I are tired and sooty. Zena regards us with interest from where she lies outside the ring of smoldering piles of charred hay and scattered metal barrels.

"Now what do we do?"

"We make sure there's nothing still on fire, and go to bed," Honora says. "Tomorrow we can dig out the pots and see how they turned out."

I'm disappointed we won't see the results of our bizarre ritual immediately. I feel intimate with it, like I've shared in its creation. Zena, familiar with the end of this dangerous activity, stands and shakes.

"No walk tonight, Zena baby," Honora says.

When I get home, it's one a.m.

6 Honora is huddled in a bathrobe at her kitchen table.

Her hands are gripping a mug of tea and her hair is in a sloppy ponytail. She offers a weak smile.

"Zena hasn't been out yet this morning," she says. Her voice cracks. "I did manage to feed her, though."

I forget all about the pottery I've hurried over to see this morning. Honora's legs are shaky when she stands to get me a tea mug.

"No, let me," I say. "You're sick."

Honora sighs.

"Sick, yes," she says. "Started puking like two hours ago." She chuckles mirthlessly.

"Tell me what you need me to take care of," I say.

"Don't you have school today?"

"No. It's Sunday."

Honora shuffles toward the kitchen door. "I'm going back to bed. Please take care of Zena? And the pottery we did last night, too."

I watch her plod down the little hallway to the parlor. I hear her unsteady feet on the stairs, followed a few minutes later by retching sounds and a toilet flushing above.

"Poor Honora." I bury my face in Zena's neck. I like the way her ear flops over my face, like a curtain, when I nuzzle her this way. "She'll be fine," I add. "Let's go for a walk."

Near the creek, I feel a few random drops of rain on my cheeks. Zena is sucking creek water between rubbery lips. When she straightens, escaping water cascades from her jowls.

Rain. Would it hurt the pottery?

"Come on, Zena, run!" I command. Panic propels my feet, and Zena falls in stride beside me. For me, an all-out sprint and stumble through the woods; for Zena, a comfortable trot.

I wish I could ride her.

How could I have left all that beautiful pottery out in the rain. What if all that hard work is ruined?

Just before I get to the back gate, the rain begins to fall with a vengeance. Raindrops collect on my eyelashes and make it hard to see. Rainwater enters my mouth, which is open and gasping. I slip on the wet grass while running full tilt across the open yard behind the gardens, but Zena's strong back is there next to me and I steady myself.

It feels good to run.

Behind the garden shed, rain is pelting the piles of charred hay. In some places, the hay is floating on top of puddles that have formed in the downpour.

"Oh, Zena, let them be okay," I plead.

I remove clumps of drenched hay to reveal the first pot. It's a bowl with a gently curving lip, about the size of a teacup. Its inside is glossy, purple-black. Even without sunlight and in this downpour, I can see it shimmer when I move it around in the palm of my hand. The purple and black each distinct, then running together and suddenly undistinguishable, depending on the angle. I think I see a hint of gold, but it's elusive and I'm not sure if my eyes are tricking me.

But the outside.

The outside is black and ugly, like a piece of half-burned firewood. The soot rubs off on my hands a little. There is no beauty below its surface.

I uncover four more pieces. All the same. I bring them into Honora's garden shed and set them on her worktable. They look like what's left in the rubble of a huge house fire, when the whole thing has burned to the ground and the TV news shows its owner pawing through the mess looking for family photo albums.

If the rain caused this result, I'm to blame. I feel such great self-loathing that I send Zena into the house with no dog biscuit, shut the door, and run all the way home in tears.

7 Rain used to have a soothing effect on me.
Before today. Before the incident of the ruined pottery.

Mom never complains that I'm not doing something with myself when it rains. I can curl up in bed all day with a book and listen to the rain pelt the window, or drip in its mournful way from the eaves, creating patternless rivulets of water on the glass.

Mom's missing, but her car's in the driveway. No note. I wrap my hair in a bathroom-towel turban and build a blanket cocoon in bed, clutching a Kleenex. This will be a day of mourning.

I will, of course, have to resign from my job.

Maybe I'll stop by occasionally and visit Zena, if it's not too awkward. This brings a fresh wave of unexpected tears to my eyes.

I read all afternoon, until I hear a car door slam in the driveway. It's Mom, and it's no longer raining.

I watch from my cocoon as Dennis lumbers out from behind the steering wheel and unlocks the car's trunk. Together, he and Mom lift out a rocking chair. Mom leans up and kisses Dennis on the lips. Then she hoists the chair and carries it to our front door.

"Andrea? Andrea?"

I reluctantly extricate myself from my cocoon.

There's some bumping against the living room walls downstairs. Then Dennis's car pulls out of the driveway. I stretch and drag myself to the top of the stairs.

"Yeah, Mom," I call. "I'm here. Just reading."

Mom's face appears over the banister. She's smiling.

"Come see the beautiful antique rocker Dennis bought me," she says. "It's just adorable. The antique show was fun."

· Never having heard my mother, or anyone else for that matter, use the words *antique show* and *fun* in the same sentence piques my curiosity. I amble down the stairs to look at the rocking chair.

Mom has already positioned it facing our coffee table. Our old recliner is shoved aside.

"It's nice, Mom, but where will we put the recliner?"

"Oh, we'll get rid of that old thing," Mom announces. "God, that thing is older than you are."

I'm stunned. Mom hasn't thrown away anything in our house for years, except back issues of *TV Guide* and microwave dinner boxes. And Dad. A short time later, Mom is on the phone with Dennis.

"Come see how cute it looks!" she says into the phone. "I'll make you dinner. Oh, and could you help me get that old recliner down to the basement?"

At least it's only going as far as the basement, I console myself.

Mom says I can only get out of dinner with her and Dennis if I have something better to do. She, of course, will be the judge of what *better* means.

"I have to let out Mrs. Menapace's dog," I say.

Mom frowns.

"I happen to know Mrs. Menapace was released from the hospital," she replies. She's wearing that accusing expression. I wonder if, ever once, I've deserved it.

"She *is* released. But she still wants me to help her out, for pay."

"How much?"

"Seventy a week."

"Seventy a week?" Mom sputters. "Someone is going to pay you seventy dollars a week to walk their dog? She must be loaded."

I shrug, and Mom lets me skip dinner. I walk to Honora's and wonder how I'll explain to Mom that after tonight, the job is over.

Honora's garden is lively with subtle sounds: small birds bathing in the puddled indents in the stone pathways; burdened leaves releasing tiny cascades of water. Water is pouring from drainpipes on the house. I stop to hold my hand beneath a drainpipe waterfall.

Honora isn't around. Zena is not at the back door. I hesitate, afraid to wake them. I go to the pottery shed. Maybe a couple of hours has changed the charred mess I've made of Honora's pots.

The ivy around the shed is glistening with raindrops. When I brush my hand against the waxy leaves, the drops slide off in a rush, dampening my sneakers. I hesitate at the door, wondering if some fairy godmother appeared while I was in bed, waving her magic wand at the pottery and making it into something beautiful. Something not ruined by me.

But the pots are sooty and ugly. I carry the worst one, a bowl, back to the house with me. It's chalky with ash that comes off on my hands, but no matter how much I handle it, this bowl is the color of used-up charcoal.

"Honora?"

My voice is timid through the porch screen. Somewhere within, but not from the kitchen, Zena whines.

"Honora?"

I decide to let myself in. Honora doesn't need to get up for me, if she's too sick to greet company. I'm not company, at least not until I quit my job to save myself the disgrace of getting fired.

Zena is at the far end of the parlor, at the foot of the stairs. She wags her tail at me a few times, then looks upstairs. Then back at me.

"She sleeping, girl?"

Since Honora's return from the hospital, the parlor has changed. The painting on the clothesline has been replaced with two new pieces: both garden scenes in different states of eruption. Eruption, because that's what Honora's real garden has done. It's now so full of life, haphazard in its design but fascinating in the way it fits together so well. If I focus on one small piece of it, it's beautiful in its own realm.

The desk is still scattered with papers, and I notice an envelope marked with the logo of St. Margaret's Hospital on top of the piles. I feel guilty without having even opened it.

Honora has also dragged out one of the piles of paintings she keeps tied up in portfolio boards by the fireplace.

It's been set on the velvet sofa, but remains secured with twine.

Zena whines, and I snap out of my reverie.

At the bottom of the stairs, I call out, "Honora?" My voice sounds so loud I feel my cheeks burn with instant embarrassment.

Zena, impatient, pushes past me to go up the first three stairs. Then she looks back at me with that doleful expression. The one that expects me to get a clue.

I have never been upstairs in Honora's house. If she had stayed longer at the hospital, it's likely I would have explored there at some point. But there'd been enough to see downstairs.

Zena lets out a sharp bark.

She continues up the stairs, turning at the top to make sure I've followed.

I have.

There's a long hallway, with more doors than I can count in a sweeping glance. Five, maybe six? They're all closed except for two—one at the end of the hallway is open enough to reveal a toilet and the end of a claw-foot bathtub. The floor is white, swirly marble. At least Honora isn't there on the floor, kneeling in front of the toilet. Not only am I not interested in seeing that action, I'm quite sure Honora would prefer I didn't see it, either. Some things are meant to be private.

The other open door is next to the bathroom. I can't see inside it.

"Honora? It's Andrea."

Zena pads down the hall to the open door. She doesn't look back when she enters the room.

"Honora? Honora?" I'm almost yelling now, because I feel panic rise in my throat like I'm about to vomit.

Still no answer.

A horrible thought crosses my mind—what if Honora is dead?

Whoever found Diego in the teachers' lounge that day must have had at least one nightmare. Maybe it plays over and over again in their mind, and they can't escape even when they wake up. It occurs to me that no one has ever mentioned who found Diego. Who bears the scars of Diego's indifference? After all, Diego had to have thought about being found after he killed himself. He had to have wondered who it would be. He had done it in the teachers' lounge to make sure a kid didn't find him. But beyond that, he just didn't care. If he had cared, he would have done it somewhere no one would find him, no one would wake up sweating in the middle of the night after seeing the empty glaze of *his* dead eyeballs behind their own sleeping lids.

For the first time, I understand why so many people think suicide is selfish.

But Honora is a different story. Honora has cancer, and I realize how little I know about cancer. I've never known anyone who had died from it. I know there are all different kinds, and you could survive some kinds, but for others it's more tricky to come out on the winning end. I have no idea which kind Honora has. The word *cancer* alone makes me shiver. How harsh and unforgiving it sounds.

It seems a little foolish to knock on the bedroom door, but I do, just in case.

Zena barks.

I swing the door wide open.

At first I don't see Honora.

The bed is mounded with white comforters and books. It has a huge gilded headboard. I think it's empty for a moment, but with a sickening feeling, I realize there's a spray of ponytail on one of the pillows.

Zena leaps onto the bed. She nuzzles something in the pillows. I'm relieved to hear a soft moan.

Not dead. Maybe dying, but not dead.

"Honora, it's me, Andrea." It's too late to tiptoe back downstairs now, even if she's fine. I walk across the room to the huge bed, trying to find Honora's face.

I say her name a few times, this time more softly. She doesn't respond. I find her face, just barely above the surface of all those blankets. It's red and swollen, a sheen of sweat on her forehead. Not dead, but surely very sick.

Zena whines, and Honora mumbles something. I pat her cheek a few times, gently, but her eyes don't flutter open.

I want to call 911. But what if this is completely normal for a cancer patient? Zena is trying to tell me this is not normal for Honora, I know that much. But what does Zena know about cancer?

Probably about as much as I do.

In the bathroom, I find a facecloth and dampen it beneath the spigot. As in the kitchen, everything about this room is old-fashioned. I ignore the sour scent of puke that wafts from the toilet.

I return to the bedroom and hold the cold cloth to Honora's face. Zena watches intently. Honora's eyelids move.

"So hot," she rasps. "So thirsty."

My heart is still pounding as I take the stairs two at a time and race through the parlor to the kitchen. I find a pitcher and a glass in the dish-drying rack. The water I get from the kitchen sink slops over onto the stairs, but I ignore it. I run.

"Honora, drink this," I whisper.

I hold the glass of water near the ponytail lying on the sheet. Honora moves her head above the comforter and squints at my hand.

"Water?" she asks.

"Yes."

Honora musters enough strength to raise up on one elbow. She greedily downs the water.

"I think you have a fever," I say. "Should I call a doctor?"

Honora's pupils are dark as she looks at me. There are crescents of blue on the skin beneath her eyes. I look away.

"They gave me the maximum dose they thought I could handle," Honora whispers and flops back onto her pillow.

"Ovarian cancer caught late," she says. "In cancer lingo, that's the equivalent of a single warrior marching into battle against an army. They've already got me surrounded.

"It appears I have two choices. Go out calm and serene, even though I'm truly panicked and alone on the inside. Or, focus every last ounce of energy on the fight."

I swallow. "Which have you chosen?"

"Well, might as well try the fight." She smiles faintly. I notice how familiar Zena is on her bed, head resting on Honora's legs. I wonder if Zena senses how terribly sick her mistress is.

"I'll need you to be my assistant in that, too," Honora says. "If at any point you become unwilling, you may be released from your employment. You need to tell me, Andrea. It could get difficult."

She yawns and smiles again. I notice her lips are dry and cracked. "Guess you already figured that out, huh?"

"I'll try," I say quietly, offering her the water glass again. It's far too unfamiliar to me, this cancer, to promise anything more than trying.

"There's a notebook and pen on the nightstand," Honora says. "I need you to take down a recipe."

"For pond-scum tea?" I ask.

Honora tries to laugh, but instead sputters into a coughing fit.

"Pretty much," she says when she's able to speak again.

8 At the bottom of Honora's staircase, I turn left.

I haven't explored this part of the house yet. I allow my eyes to adjust to the dimness of a formal entry. Instead of a place for greeting guests at a cocktail party, it's a place of stacking. There are books, baskets, bundles of newspapers, some empty picture frames propped in a dusty corner.

The formal entry narrows into a dark hallway. Halfway down is a small coatroom. Beyond that is a door.

Through the door I find another parlor. This one is more lavish than the one where Honora keeps her paintings. It's obviously an unused room. I shudder at its museum feeling, despite elegant sofas and chairs, poised as if waiting for company that never came. Beyond this parlor is the dining room. Just as Honora instructed, there's a sliding pocket door about halfway down the dark wood walls.

I skirt my way around the dining table. There are sixteen chairs surrounding it.

I bet Mom would love to have Dennis haul that dining set back from some antique show. Remove the back wall of our house and it would fit just fine.

I slide the pocket door open.

A cold pantry, Honora had called it.

The last of the day's sunlight streams through a single dusty window that's some two feet above my head. It smells like dirt and Arabian spices, incense and dust. A ladder leans against the wall just to the left of the window. Above my head are hundreds of bound and inverted dried plants, tacked to the dark timbers that line the ceiling. There are three enormous sets of apothecary drawers, a heavy butcher-block table in the center of the room, and stacks and stacks of spiral-bound notebooks.

The floor is nothing more than dinner-plate-sized slabs of slate, caulked together with what looks like mud. There are two doors, one probably leading to the kitchen, the other leading outside. I see a little kerosene lamp on the butcher block, which I notice is pockmarked with knife gouges. I light the lamp and flatten my sheet of notebook paper on the battered surface of the butcher block.

Hypericum
Verbana
Melissa
White dead nettle

Honora had also written down the exact quantities of each herb. I read the list out loud, twice. I like the melodic, foresty sound of the herbs.

After I remove vials of mysterious ingredients from tiny, labeled drawers in the apothecary chest, I measure the perfect amounts using a teaspoon. Engraved on its handle are a moon, a sun, and a star. Taped to the drawers are handwritten labels. WILD CHERRY BARK. WHITE HORE-HOUND. WHITE DEAD NETTLES.

The last one makes me think about Diego, dead and lying in his cemetery plot in Patriotsville, Ohio. Funny, how I associate the herb with death because of its name, when Honora associates it with life.

I make Honora's tea mixture, clamping it all together and encasing it in a metal mesh tea ball. I'm nervous. What if just an extra granule caused convulsions?

Honora is sitting up in bed when I make it back to her room. She's stroking Zena's ears.

"Ah, lovely." She nods. "Thank you."

I set the mug of steaming tea in her outstretched hands, and she smiles gratefully.

"Do you have time to walk Zena?"

Zena's ears perk.

"I do, but there's something I have to tell you."

I take a deep breath.

"I left the pottery out in the rainstorm," I confess. "It's ruined."

I stand there, ashamed, and wait for Honora's anger and dismay. I wait for her eyes to register what has happened, for her to realize that I had destroyed her art. She would have no choice but to allow me to slink back into the obscurity from which I had come.

Assistant, fired.

Pathetic Nothing Andrea Anderson, dismissed from Honora's life. And Zena's.

Instead, Honora laughs.

"Everyone thinks the phoenix rises from the ashes, gleaming and unscathed. Until they know better."

Honora takes a long draw on her tea, then settles back against her pillows.

"Andrea Anderson, you will see."

ACT

4

1 Monday.

Homeroom is deflated, like each of us students got dropped into an all-new high school and had to reinvent ourselves. Mr. Ferris tells us he can't hang around this morning, so everyone should just sit in their seats until the bell rings.

Oddly, that's just what we do.

There's no talking, just listless waiting. Then the bell rings, and we have purpose again.

Ashley offers me another ride home from school.

"Mom gives me the minivan on Mondays and Fridays," she explains, tucking a notebook under her arm. "Bryan drives me the other days."

I accept the ride.

"I'm thinking about getting my license," I tell Ashley.

We walk in comfortable silence across the student parking lot. The lot is foreign to me, and I feel like Ashley is my well-respected wilderness guide. The Goths, the Smokers, the Class-Skippers, the Athletes, and the Drug Dealers are gathered in packs around cars, carrying out their own little performances. A fat senior is walking ahead of us, her head down, hugging an armload of books.

There are a lot of Mom minivans in the parking lot. There are also a lot of rich-kid cars and middle-class lucky-kid cars. There are plenty of tragically ugly fifty-dollar cars, most often approached by a vocational center kid with a knack for fixing.

I see Bryan Davenport's gleaming sports car in the last row.

"Why don't you ride with Bryan every day?" I ask Ashley.

Ashley gives a sultry smile to some football players, then lowers her face to my ear.

"It's the car. It's so flashy, it's embarrassing. It's worse than a Mom-i-van."

I snort and consider the irony of this. Half of Simmonsville High School despised Ashley for the Four Gifts of B: her beauty, her body, her brains, and her boyfriend. Even a bad haircut hadn't been enough to detract from Ashley's gifts. She had it all and she never seemed to work for any of it.

And she was ungrateful.

I'm stunned.

"Ashley, why are you being so nice to me?" I ask suddenly. "You don't need to be, you know."

Ashley side-steps a carload of goody girls, smiling benignly at the hopeful faces they turn her way.

"Maybe that's just it," Ashley says. "Maybe it's because I don't need you. I've been taught that I need popular friends, need a hot boyfriend, need good grades for cheerleading. Which, by the way, basically equates to a need for a great social life. I've been taught that crap since third grade.

"And right now, I need to find out what life is like outside of such superficial values. Because it's all nothing."

Ashley sweeps her arm to encompass the football field and Bryan Davenport's car.

"It's not me. I need a damn intermission from it all so I can take a break. My life just turned out this way, and this way is so incredibly boring and competitive and frivolous, I need a break."

Ashley gulps for air, then lets out a long breath. When she speaks again, her voice is shaky.

"I have to stop by my dad's work and pick up the mutts for him. I can either drop you off at your house, or you can come along and meet the flea motels since you're a dog fan, too."

Sure, I could.

Before I can answer, Ashley unlocks the Mom-i-van. In the car next to us, a pack of pot smokers has already lit up a joint. Another performance completely. Sullen white faces beneath sloppy skater hairstyles, and black T-shirts. No one ever seems to know their names. All the clean kids are scared of them, because what is it like to alter your mind?

One of the pot smokers smiles wide at Ashley from the backseat of the car, daring her to smile back. He places a finger to his lips, kisses it, and points at her. The other palefaces in the kingdom of the pot-smokers' car contort with laughter I can't hear through the rolled-up windows.

Act 4—Pot Smokers Ridicule Cheerleader.

Ashley unlocks the Mom-i-van and puts on her yearbook smile. I stifle a giggle when she raises her middle finger at them.

"Kiss that!" Ashley shouts when we're safely inside the Mom-i-van. I refuse to look at the car of pot smokers as we pull out of our parking spot, but I imagine their faces are either stunned or amused, beneath a veil of smoke.

Ashley drives.

I giggle.

Ashley's dad's office is a little corrugated metal building behind a warehouse. It's in the part of town where train tracks riddle the streets. Most buildings are empty, glass long smashed from window frames. There's a diner truck stop and a parking lot full of town highway department trucks.

Ashley double-checks to make sure the van is in park before she taps the horn. Almost immediately, the door on the little building swings open and three dogs charge out.

"Picking the kids up from day care!" she hollers out the window to the man who hangs partway out the door and waves to us. Ashley hops out and opens the sliding side door of the minivan, and the three dogs leap in. They jostle each other for the spot where their heads can reach the hands of the humans in the front seat.

"Meet Dursee, Tralee, and Killarney," Ashley says, hopping in. "More affectionately known as Dirt, Tray, and Kooky Monster. Not Cookie, Kooky. Imagine having to shout 'Kooky Monster' out the back door at night for all the neighbors to hear."

I burst out laughing. Kooky is the Newfoundland, fur like a yak, barrel-nosed and saggy-lipped.

Within seconds of getting in the van, Kooky leaves a damp stain of drool on the shoulder of my T-shirt.

"Kooky," admonishes Ashley, dabbing at my shoulder.

"Kooky, you can drool on me anytime you please," I say. Ashley laughs.

"You know, that's how my family feels about him, too." Each dog settles with its haunches on the middle seat of the van, and there's a chorus of panting and jangling collars behind us.

"I've never met a Newfoundland before," I say, turning sideways to look at Kooky Monster. He's nearly as big as Zena, but he lacks her sleek dignity. He has kinky fur and black spots on his foamy tongue.

"People who love Newfoundlands usually just call them Newfies," Ashley says, glancing sidelong at Kooky's damp muzzle on her headrest. "Newfoundland is just too formal for a dog that's more like a giant teddy bear."

We take the dogs to a park. Ashley and I throw sticks and make fun of the Newfy trying to keep up with the two agile Labs.

"You still taking care of some old lady's Saint?" Ashley asks, breaking a stick in half over her knee and leaving a streak of dirt on her jeans.

"Actually, she's not that old after all," I answer. "And yeah, I'm her assistant now."

I realize I've been Honora's assistant for four days, and Ashley is the first person I'm telling. I tell her more about Zena, Honora, the pottery, the cancer, the gardens, the tea herbs. I leave out the ruined raku.

"I don't know much about the herbs yet. She's teaching me. Right now, I just like the names. Anise, balm of Gilead, yellow wild indigo."

Ashley tries out the last one, allowing it to roll slow and ripe from her lips.

"Yellow wild indigo."

I smile.

Ashley is interested. Interested in something I have offered.

Me, Andrea Anderson.

2 Zena greets me at the back gate.

Honora is in her garden, bent over a plot of dirt as if she hadn't been half-dead just the day before. She's wearing something she calls a yoga robe, but the rest of the world calls a bathrobe. When she looks up to smile at me, her eyes look rheumy.

"Ah, it is Andrea," she announces. "Straight-up chamomile today, or would you prefer some of the gacky-tasting stuff?"

"I'll take a short-order of gack," I say. "But only if you tell me what's in it. And how it works."

Honora nods. She goes indoors to prepare the tea while I scratch Zena's rump.

"This is a traditional Ojibwa native tea," Honora says as she sets a tray on the top porch step. She strains the herb-and-root mixture from the brown liquid and pours it into my glass.

"Promotes general detoxification, which basically means cleans you out. Removes impurities in your blood, your kidneys. Burdock root, red clover, slippery elm, blessed thistle, a few other things for taste."

I sip from my glass and wince. Honora chuckles and drinks hers without flinching.

"Come to the shed," she says.

The ruined pottery is spaced along Honora's worktable

145

in a perfect row. Honora fetches a large utility lantern from the corner of the shed and drags it into the center of the space. Once it's plugged in, it sheds a warming glow over the worktable.

"Moon glow," Honora says. "Not quite as golden as the color of light from the sun, it has more white and blue to it. It's all in the lighting, what we see."

I think about walking in the woods late at night, the shadows grasping at the ankles of every tree. Each shadow, as you train your eyes, becomes unique; not quite the same shade of gray or black, sometimes a tinge of mossy purple playing at the edges. These places can be deep or shallow, and your eyes try to ascertain, but are left wanting. It's from there that fear comes, that inability to see, but sometimes it can be exhilarating and beautiful.

A stoneware bowl of cold water is placed on the worktable, and Honora hands me a nubbly sponge and a canister of Ajax.

"Just scrub," she says simply. "Scrub hard enough to set the colors free."

Honora leaves, and I feel a tiny pang of jealousy as Zena pads out behind her mistress. But then I'm drawn to the pottery.

As I scrub Ajax on the first piece, a vase, I worry that I'll scrub too hard and ruin it twice. The sooty surface doesn't come off easily, though. Then, when I'm feeling hopeless and betrayed, it comes: a streak of rich green marble, like gold beneath the layers of earth.

3 Roger Dupris is shooting hoops in his driveway. The dusk has turned too heavy to see the net. He's alone, and pauses to give me a quick wave.

"Hey, Andrea."

"Hey."

I pause at the end of his driveway, wondering if the ecstasy in my heart is enough to do it. To call out to him without fear of cruel laughter, even though he's never once been cruel before.

"Roger, want to see something?" My voice is pinched. I feel reckless.

Roger dribbles down his driveway, then tucks the basketball beneath his elbow. He sees me huddle protectively over what it is that I'm holding.

He waits. I unfurl the vase that Honora has given me away from my chest, where I've been hugging it to protect it from my own exhilaration.

I'm disappointed when I realize that it's too dark to see.

"It's a vase that I rakued," I say.

"What does that mean?" Roger is interested, and this gives me courage.

"You burn it in a fire, after you put on ceramic glazes. You can't see it in the dark, but it's got all these amazing shades of color on it. Swirled and light and dark and . . ."

147

My voice trails off. "I'll just show it to you sometime when it's light, I guess."

Roger takes a step back, his eyes still on the vase.

"Why don't you show it to me now? The front porch has a light."

I follow Roger stupidly up his driveway. What had started out as a quick show of the vase, a casual act of friendliness, has just turned into a committed death march to the light of Roger's porch. I feel foolish. We don't speak until after Roger flicks on the porch light and looks.

"Andrea, that's so awesome," Roger says while I hold my breath. "I can't believe you made that. Can I touch it?"

I feel relief and pride wash over my face, then feel foolish again, thinking of how the nerd next to me in homeroom looked when I accepted his intrusions. Here *I* was doing it. But I hold the vase out to Roger anyway.

"I didn't make the vase, or even paint it with the glaze," I say. "I just set it on fire."

Roger laughs and without thinking I do too.

4 Gimelli's Shop and Run is having a special on toilet paper.

I buy an extra roll. After Mrs. Gimelli hands me my change, I study the fluorescent lights, suspended from the ceiling in corrugated metal chandeliers.

On my walk home, I cut through the park past the water fountain. It's surrounded by a concrete ramp and railing, and Wendy Cartwright's little brother Paul is there, skateboarding with his friends.

Wendy's little brother used to be a chubby kid who pedaled his Big Wheel furiously around the cul-de-sac. Now he's lanky and sullen, with too-white arms jutting from a black T-shirt and carelessly tied sneakers.

Paul watches me openly as I make my way past. I use my arm to hide the SUPPORT YOUR LIBRARY slogan on my canvas bag as best I can. I'm wary. I sense he's going to say something, and sure enough it comes.

"Hey, why are you going up to Old Lady Menapace's place so much?" he shouts at me. His tone isn't friendly, or even that curious. "You know, she's a nut job. Crazy."

I shrug and focus on the sidewalk. Two mashed-out cigarette butts. A crumpled dandelion that has crept between the cracks.

Paul's friends have stopped skating. Nervously, I glance at them. They have all cocked their skateboards beneath one foot and are staring at me, smirking. I go back to staring at the sidewalk and concentrating on how I walk. Keep it casual, not too fast. They're younger than you, surely that counts for an ounce of respect?

"You're a nut job, too," Paul hollers. "You're like some fifty-year-old lady who lives with her cats."

The friends snigger a little. I'm almost far enough away to let down my guard a little, but not quite.

I think about turning around and yelling something back. Instead I trip over a crack in the sidewalk and stumble just enough to drop my SUPPORT YOUR LIBRARY canvas bag.

The toilet paper rolls out, catching itself on the grass edging where the concrete sidewalk ends.

Just my luck.

5 Honora prepares us two glasses of yarrow tea. I notice she's pale and keeps clearing her throat. Zena bounds happily in the garden, which has now sprouted lemon-yellow and lavender flowers. A new row of tulips has appeared along the stone walkway next to the veranda. Honora calls them black beauties.

"They're really kind of dark purple, right?" I say.

"Almost black, but almost purple."

Honora smiles.

"If you ever get the chance to look closely at an African person's skin in the right light, a person whose skin is very dark, you can see tinges of purple," she says. "It's a rich, exquisite thing."

Honora drains her glass. I brace myself for the acrid taste of dirt and moss, but the yarrow is bland. I drink it quickly.

"Come here and look at something." Honora stands. She walks over to the bed of tulips and lies down on her back in the middle of them. I watch as she settles her head in the dirt carefully, avoiding the flowers it holds.

"Come here and check this out."

I go and lie down next to Honora. The swaying tulips brush my cheeks and the place where the stalks intersect the bottom of each flower is the only view of the world I have.

"Now, just look."

Honora becomes silent.

I lie there and look at the undersides of the flowers, the fragile veins connecting the stems to the graceful curve of the petals.

"Isn't it amazing how many viewpoints of our world there are, and how rarely we look?" Honora says finally.

She stands, and I get up slowly to avoid damaging the tulips.

Honora goes inside to paint while I walk Zena. When I drop Zena off, Honora is bent over her easel and doesn't look at me.

"Are you free Saturday?" she calls. "I'd like you to go with me on my rounds. The galleries, the art store, the natural-food store."

"How's ten o'clock?" I ask.

"Wonderful."

On Saturday, Mom and Dennis leave early for yet another antique show.

As if one wasn't enough for them.

At least this thing they have for antique shows solves the problem of explaining to Mom where I'll be all day. I'm eager to spend a day running errands with Honora.

When I get to her house, Honora is on the back porch.

She's fiddling with cardboard boxes and packing peanuts. Zena lies on the grass, tail thumping.

"I like your scarf," I say as I approach. It's scarlet, with tiny specks of mirrors sewn at its edges with gold thread.

"It's a Roma headpiece," Honora says, touching her palm to the tightly wrapped scarf. "Roma are Gypsies from Eastern Europe."

"Like fortune-tellers?"

"Some, yes. Others, no."

I hold the flaps of one of the cardboard boxes open while Honora adjusts the finished pottery inside. She tucks packing peanuts between each piece. In addition to the headpiece, she's wearing blue jeans and a white linen blouse. Gothic-looking bracelets hang from her skinny wrists.

"There's only going to be four boxes today, I think," she says, straightening up. "We're going to hit two galleries in Talcottville and one down in Lakes County. Tea?"

"Maybe when we get back," I answer. "Should I walk Zena before we go?"

"Yes. And I could use a walk, too."

Zena rises and stretches expectantly. Honora leaves the boxes on the porch and we head toward the gate at the back of her lawn.

"Walking tires me out, but I'd like to take a look at the wild yarrow plants. The nettles should be looking healthy by now, too."

Despite her illness, Honora walks purposefully. Zena darts ahead and snuffles her great nose into ferns and rotting leaves. At the ridge overlooking the creek, Honora cuts off the path and heads for a rock overhang.

"This is one of my hangouts," she says. "It's a rest stop on the highway."

We sit on the rock, hugging our knees. the creek is languid from lack of rain, and Zena trots down the steep embankment and splashes in. She drinks heavily and snorts. Honora laughs.

"There's a mountain in the Adirondacks," Honora says. "It's called Saddleback. At three thousand feet, there's a rock like this. You can sit and stare out over wilderness and time. It feels like there's nothing taller than you, and like the wind might sweep you free like a particle of dust at any minute, while you're just sitting there being microscopic."

I no longer feel awkward and second-rate with Honora. I've realized that I'm one color in her painting of the world. And while any artist may have her favorite colors, a good artist never discredits those subtle, shy hues that contribute to the landscape.

Zena pauses in her ascent of the ravine wall to check a mossy log. She's wet on her underside and legs, making her look shaggy on top and sleek on the bottom. The perfect brown disk on the top of her head is smeared with dirt and moss.

"How did you get Zena?" I ask.

Honora laughs.

"She was a gift from a man you'll meet today, Hughie Nye," she says. "He's a gallery owner I've worked with for years. About four years ago I walked into his place, and there he is, holding out this fat puppy.

"Seems this couple came into his gallery and proceeded to have a very public argument about the puppy. The husband had bought it for the wife, and the wife probably wanted some yappy dog she could dress up in St. Patrick's Day sweaters and yellow plastic raincoats. Definitely not a huge, drooling beast. Anyway, Hughie spoke up for the puppy and Zena got dumped off then and there. Hughie remembered I always had dogs around, so when I walked in later that same day, he offered her to me."

"I never get tired of watching her," I say.

"Me neither." Honora smiles and stands up, offering me her hand. We stand on the rock overlooking the creek, our feet as close to the overhang as we dare place them.

"There's some yarrow," she says, pointing. The weeds and plants all look the same to me, but Honora has spied it easily among the collage of greens.

Honora adjusts her Roman head scarf, so that the tiny mirrors glitter briefly, like fireflies.

"Zena, come!" she calls.

Zena, who usually reports directly when called, is frozen next to the moss-covered log. Her ears are cocked and her nose is focused on the top of the steep ridge facing us, on the other side of the creek. I look at the ridge line and gasp.

"Honora, a coyote," I whisper. I feel the hairs on my arms prickle. The coyote's coat is matted and bristly. Its snout is pointed. Its eyes are locked on Zena.

"A morning sighting," Honora says quietly. "I bet she has babies nearby."

"Will Zena be okay?" I ask. I'm both anxious and elated. It's an amazing feeling, to become suddenly aware of such an elusive wild animal, watching you. I knew enough about the woods to know a coyote wouldn't attack a human, or even a dog the size of Zena. But to be the object of scrutiny by a predator is strangely exhilarating.

"She's fine. She's much more aware of the contents of this moment than we are. Just watch."

I glance at Honora, still nervous. My beautiful Zena, in a fight with a coyote. But a tiny smile has formed at the edges of Honora's mouth. It's the smile of gradually realizing the magnitude of an event's meaning. Honora looks beautiful. I see then that her Gypsy scarf has tilted over her forehead, exposing bald scalp above her right ear. I'll remind her to fix it before we get in the car.

Then I smile, too.

The coyote's nostrils flare in the breeze with interest. As minutes pass and we stare at each other, its interest seems to wane. We've become less threatening, just by doing nothing. The coyote settles on its haunches and glances away.

"Brand-new babies," Honora says. "She's checking on them. Look for chewed-away fur on her belly. Then we'll know she's a new mom."

Zena, too, has sat down on the awkward incline of the ravine wall. Her sturdy white forelegs are holding her steady on the loose earth.

"No fur on her belly," Honora points out.

Then the coyote is gone, into the bushes without so much as a crack of twigs or a ruffle of leaves.

The main road out of Simmonsville fades behind Honora's old gray van as I watch out the side-view mirror. We have the windows rolled down, and Honora's boxes of pottery are on the floor behind our seats, along with a cardboard cake box sealed with masking tape.

"Road trips aren't really meant to efficiently connect two points on a map," Honora explains, turning onto a pot-holed country road that leads over the Simmons county line.

Simmonsville should have been named Nowheresville, Pennsylvania. There are dozens of county routes and old farmer's roads that lead someplace important to somebody. There are sudden intersections with four or five houses clumped around them for no apparent reason. There are miles of vacant land and farm fields. Tiny hamlets look lonesome alongside metal signs declaring them worthy of existing. Signs like Wampsville and Macomb Corners.

"Have you thought any more about your driver's permit?" Honora asks.

Her wrapped-up head is lolling peacefully on the headrest. She's used the rearview mirror to correct her scarf, without any prompting from me. I try to imagine her completely bald. No graceful bun fixed with Japanese painted hairpins or a set of worn-out paintbrushes. I feel guilty for my curiosity into her privacy.

I don't tell her that my mother will probably disapprove of the whole driver's permit thing.

"I think I'll go to the motor vehicle office and pick up a study guide," I say. "Maybe even this week."

Honora nods.

We drive.

"I spent a summer, during grad school, driving myself and my husband up to Northern Quebec," she says. "Three weeks driving in some of the most remote, breathtaking land I've ever seen. One time, the road we were on for hours was so narrow, you hit scrub brush on both sides of the car while you were driving along. I kept wondering what you did if you came to another car head-on. We traveled one hundred miles on the same road, and never did see another car."

Honora smiles.

"We stopped right in the middle of that road and made tea. Boiled water on a little propane grill, steeped the tea, and drank it, with our car parked right in the middle of the road, all the doors open."

I watch out the window. A small boy is playing with a homely dog in the yard of a mobile home, laughing and jostling the dog for the stick in its mouth.

We are about a half hour outside Simmonsville. I don't really recognize anything. I think about how little I know about the places that Mom hasn't driven me to for her own needs, or the places I can walk to myself.

I think about Dad. Where had he gone? Had he ended up along one of these country roads, living inside one of the houses we passed? Or had he moved on to a city, started a new family? It was too late for him to be anything but a stranger to me. But I was curious about him. To see what kind of smile he had now, or what he kept in his coat pockets, or which flavor ice cream he chose from the freezer. Were we anything alike, or would we have gotten along about as badly as me and Mom, if he had stayed in my life?

Honora slows the van and turns on her signal in front of an ancient farmhouse with dark, gaping windows. The paint is peeling and the front porch is stacked with hay.

"Is this a gallery?" I ask stupidly.

Honora unclasps her seat belt and pats my arm.

"Like I said, road trips are an adventure."

8 The woman who answers the door and leads us inside to her cluttered kitchen introduces herself as Daria.

Like Honora, she gently cups my face in her palms. I try not to go rigid.

"Andrea," she says softly. Her smile is warm and I feel humbled by the wisdom in her voice, the way she speaks and looks at me. I see tiny specks of purple in her gray pupils; the creases of wrinkles below her eyelashes look like they've been forged by a constant breeze.

Daria is wearing green slippers and a faded peasant dress. Her hair is gray and white and unruly. Her face is scarred with sun spots and moles, but she seems unashamed of them; as though they're just the marks of having lived a life outdoors.

As gently as she placed her hands on my face, she removes them and greets Honora.

"Nora, I see things have not been all well for you," Daria says. "You need some spring vegetables and some cinnamon-basil honey."

Honora hugs Daria and places her head, briefly, on the woman's shoulder. I look away, at the worn-out wood floors, the picnic-bench dinner table stacked with papers and oddities: a box of roofing nails, a laundry basket, and three spider plants.

"Traveling a little does me wonders," Honora says. "It's good for the soul to smell springtime."

"Of course it is," Daria says. "I've prepared a vegetable strain for you. My grandmother's recipe. Andrea, would you like to try some? It's a powerful boost of vitamins, a healthy pulse of energy, some say."

Honora accepts the steaming cup from Daria. Daria dips the spoon back into the iron kettle on her stovetop and offers it to me.

"It tastes a bit like eating raw earth, molten lava," she says. "My grandmother was an herbal doctor in a remote part of East Germany, before they erected the Berlin Wall. She was there when the Wall was built. She died while the Wall was still in place.

"She lived on a sheep farm some seventy miles from the Wall. But the Wall was there, and they had little influence from the outside world. They had no village doctor. Women filled those roles back then."

A cat peers doubtfully at me from on top of a stack of kitchen towels. Daria sets a mug for me on the picnic table. Then she spoons herself some.

"My grandma was their first line of medical care. For every ailment a neighbor might have, she had an herbal remedy. And she was just a sheep farmer's wife with an affinity for plants and herbs."

Daria extends a spoon in my direction.

"Here, just give it a taste and see what you think."

The spoon's contents look like slimy iguana skin.

"It's just the usual fruits and vegetables you would eat every day. You extract the parts with the most potency, then puree it to mash. A few run-of-the-mill herbs in there, too."

I place the spoon in my mouth. The taste is jarring, like I've stuffed my mouth full with the filth you find under a front porch. Dead leaves and wet dirt.

I smile bravely. I don't want another taste.

Honora laughs. Daria and I do, too.

Daria tells me her workshop used to be in the barn. But since she's gotten older, she's moved her workshop onto the closed-in back porch of the farmhouse, where weeds grow beneath the walls like unexpected guests and cracked windows are repaired with duct tape.

"This way, I get to avoid carrying every darn piece back down from the barn at night to keep it warm," Daria says. "I used to do that. Then I'd haul it back on up there to the barn the next day. I just can't manage the cold the way I used to. I used to thrive in it, that focus you get when your body is really working to stay warm and healthy."

Honora nods. "I don't think I have it in me as much to tend my raku pit," she says. "Andrea is working half the shift with me, doing the puff and snuff."

"Ah," Daria says to me. "Exhilarating, isn't it? There's something quite ceremonial about it."

I smile and look around at Daria's workshop.

Daria is a wood turner. Scraps of hollowed-out logs, husks of wood shavings are knee-deep around a huge metal tool propped on steel legs in the center of the porch.

"A lathe," Honora says to me.

Daria unscrews a metal plate holding her current piece on the lathe. She sets it on the floor and screws a different metal plate into the end of a fresh log. Then she hoists it onto her belly and screws it in place on the lathe.

"These are the lathe tools." She shows me a tray of wood-handled tools, some with thick, sharp tips and others with blunt, curled tips.

They are basically the gouges, she says. They chisel away the surface of the wood until you get the effect you want. If you gouge the entire outside of the log, line by line by line, then you have the outside surface of a vase, a goblet, a bowl, you name it.

"The wood tells you what to do," Daria says. "Most of the time, it knows what shape it's meant to be better than you do. You just listen to it, and gouge it out. It comes off in peels.

"My granddaughter visited me a few years back. I let her give it a try, and she said it was like a video game because the wood spins so fast on the lathe. I've never played a video game in my life, so I'll have to take her word on that."

Daria dusts off a plastic face mask that looks like something either a beekeeper or an astronaut might wear. When she guides it over my head, I feel like I've just put on a Halloween costume. For a moment I relish that feeling, of being someone other than myself for one night. Someone outlandish and accepted.

Daria positions me in front of the lathe. She stands behind me with her hands on top of mine, moving my fingers to the right places on one of the wood gouges.

"Okay, I'm going to turn it on." Daria taps a switch on

the floor with her left green slipper. "Resist the urge to let it come up toward your face, but not too forcefully or you'll ruin the piece. It's a balancing act for thrill seekers. If you can't yo-yo perfectly between creating your piece and nearly gouging your face with a tool, you've lost the balance."

My hands are limp under Daria's, until the lathe's machinery whirrs to life, and the log begins spinning. It has a dreamy quality, this hum of machinery and a log swirling. Daria's hands guide mine to the surface of the log. When the tool strikes wood, the speed of the log makes it jump in my hands. Daria forces my hands to resist this rebuff. A slice of pristine wood begins to appear amid the craggy bark.

I'm mesmerized.

Daria continues to direct the tool in my awkward hands, and thin peels of wood and bark gather at our feet. When Daria eventually turns off the lathe, we stand in the sudden silence and admire our work. I look at the wood we've revealed: fresh, pale yellow; random streaks of brown and gray mottling its surface.

"Not bad for a start." Daria releases her grip on my hands. "What did the wood tell you to make?"

I rub my hands to relieve the strange sensation from the vibration of the machinery. I look at Daria's gentle smile.

"Maybe a candlestick?"

My words are more of an anxious question than anything else.

Honora smiles with encouragement.

"I love the look of burgundy candle wax cascading down a candlestick made of black cherrywood," Honora says. "Lovely."

She turns to Daria.

"We should be going."

"I'm reluctant to let you go," Daria answers, resting her palm on Honora's cheek.

Before leaving, we make three trips to the van with boxes of Daria's bowls and vases. The smell of wood varnish fills the van.

Daria hugs me in her kitchen and hands Honora a canning jar full of the foul liquid she had served earlier.

"Warm it good before you drink it, Nora. That way you'll release the aromas and mingle them, plus hot foods go down easier than cold."

"I love you, Daria."

"I love you too, my friend."

Honora pulls the van into the gravel parking lot of Pocono Mountain Art, Inc.

There are no other cars there. The front porch of the shop is littered with wrought-iron statues and obelisks. The shop's sign is propped on a rocking chair next to the front door.

It's definitely the type of place my mother would never have entered. I imagine her sniffing in disgust at someone's art, or its price.

"Christ, haven't these people heard of Wal-Mart?" she'd growl.

Honora twists over her seat to size up the boxes in the back of the van.

"Are you sure someone's here?" I ask.

"Oh, I'm sure."

Honora instructs me to carry one of Daria's boxes. She picks up a cake box from the floor.

On the gallery's front door, a handwritten sign is taped to the glass.

COME WELL. COME HAPPY.

PLEASE RING THE BELL

TO TELL ME YOU HAVE COME.

167

Honora presses the doorbell next to the sign. It doesn't ring and she chuckles.

With one elbow, she gently opens the gallery door and we step inside.

"James?" she calls politely.

I look around the gallery. Pieces of art, some medieval, some contemporary, are erupting from shelves and walls and even the ceiling. Handwoven rugs with price tags are scattered on the floor in places you wouldn't be likely to step on them. All the art is tagged with an ecru-colored index card, describing the work, the artist, and finally, the price.

"James?"

Honora is making her way, at a slow pace, toward a desk at the back of the shop. The gallery seems museumlike to me as I wait by the door, a museum my mother would say was a tribute to useless industry. I imagine her sneering about the foolishness of art and Gloria agreeing, mindlessly.

But I love Pocono Mountain Art, Inc.

Mirabelle Hough, textiles. $400. Cascade Hill Pottery, urn. $185.

All these beautiful people, making things and selling them here. I wonder who buys them. I wonder how they can fully enjoy them, being so disconnected with their creators.

Honora places the cake box on the desk and turns to me, holding a finger to her lips. Then she beckons me forward.

I find James, as Honora has already found him, curled under a quilt. He's lying on a battered velvet sofa, the kind intended for Victorian ladies in tent-bottom dresses. Certainly not a drooling man in a concert tour shirt from 1979. The sofa is just behind the cash register. A tortoise-shell cat is flicking its tail, silently, from its perch on the sofa's arm.

Honora grins at me. She takes the box from my arms and sets it down. Then she tears a sheet of paper from an empty pad on James's desk. We both cringe and stifle giggles at the sudden, loud sound of paper tearing free. While she writes James a note, I look at him.

James is probably in his forties, with horn-rimmed glasses still propped on his nose even in sleep. The lenses of the glasses are thick and confusing. He has a handsome face. His lips are parted just slightly, the hint of a snore wheezing between them.

Honora finishes her note and places it on top of the cake box.

"We have to bring one of my boxes in there," she says as we giggle our way back to the van. "I'll do it. That cat is probably going to eat right through the cake box before James wakes up." Honora laughs.

"What's in it?" I ask.

"Just some lavender cookies. James is a bachelor, so getting a plate of homemade cookies is quite the prize."

"Do you make them out of real lavender?" I wrinkle my nose.

"Lavender petals, minced up small. Lovely taste."

Honora conducts the stealth mission to drop off the second box. When she hops back in the van, she's still smirking.

"I would have liked you to meet James, though," she says, starting up the van. "He's quite the character, but I know him well enough not to wake him up. He's coming down off a manic."

"What?"

"James is manic-depressive. Real high highs, where he works with precision and genius for days straight, not sleeping and barely eating. Then low lows, where he sleeps for days and even changing his clothes becomes a real struggle. He's clearly on a low. You should meet him on a high, though. What a genius."

"Isn't there a cure or a medicine?" I ask.

Honora shrugs.

"James is content with it. His friends tend to think of it as a personality trait, not a mental illness. Drugs might make him more normal, I suppose. But how many interesting people do you know who are really trying to be normal?"

I think about Diego. Maybe there had been more to him than I realized. Maybe there had been more to the circumstances of his death than I had allowed myself to consider.

"Well, I guess no one," I say.

"Me neither," Honora says.

10 We stop for lunch in Brewster Township. We sit on pock-holed plastic bench seats in Bev's Diner, chasing ice cubes around the inside of our water glasses with bendy straws.

The waitress is dressed like a hospital worker. Her hair's in a net, and she wears white nursing clogs over her opaque white stockings like Mom does at the hospital. Sensible shoes for long days spent on tired feet.

"Specials are the bacon-bagel sandwich, two ninety-five. Corned-beef open-faced sandwich, four ninety-five with fries."

Honora orders scrambled eggs and cherry pie. I get the cheeseburger fantasy.

"This place reminds me of where I lived as a little girl," Honora says. "My uncle Barry ran a diner, and my mom waitressed there while I was at school. When school let out, I would walk to the diner and meet my mom. She always quit working the minute I walked in."

"Is your mom still alive?" I ask.

"Nah, she loved Carlton cigarettes too much. She got lung cancer and died when she was fifty-one. What a woman she was, juggling so many balls and she never did let them drop. Except one."

Our lunches arrive. We eat in thoughtful silence. A man in work boots studies the newspaper to the left of his soup bowl at the diner counter. The cook, just behind the wait-resses' alley, yells, "Hey there, Dizzy!" at an old man who's wiping the soles of his loafers on the rug just inside the door. Dizzy nods and smiles. The waitresses are gathered at the soda machine, trying to recall which new store was opening at the mall. And Honora and I are there, part of the landscape, two friends eating comfortable food at a chipped Formica table.

11 Hughie Nye has a gallery next door to the Historical Society of the Amish Country, so it draws a lot more browsers and buyers than most galleries. The gallery is the former estate mansion of some governor or senator, Honora says. Inside, it's perfectly ordered. The floorboards creak as though complaining of the many decades of footsteps it has endured; lush Oriental carpets muffle the groans. There's intricate woodwork at the base and top of each wall, a mahogany staircase swirls down to a landing which has been chained off. NO ADMITTANCE, written in tiny, polite text.

To the left of the main hall is a great room. The shades have been drawn and bright white light is pouring from dozens of fixtures along the whitewashed walls.

Spaced at equal height along the walls are gilt-framed paintings. Each painting has its own light fixture directly above it, playing on its surface like a spotlight on a stage.

"Unlike James, Hughie is a minimalist," Honora says as we stop and gaze at the first painting. "No distractions when you enter a room. It is a disservice to the piece if it must compete with furniture and shadows and other pieces."

We wander the room separately, in silence.

My favorite painting in the room is an oil painting. It shows three children, huddled in ragged coats, facing a man driving a harvester through a cornfield. The oldest child is a boy, leaning on a fence post, focused on the progress of the harvester. The two younger children are girls, close in age. One is tucking her cheek against her collar, her feet cocked inward and turned on their sides. The other girl is smiling at a tiny spiderweb built on the fence post.

A plastic-encased card is affixed to the wall below the painting. *Autumn Spiderweb. Esther Phelps, Bradbury, Pennsylvania. $1,300.*

"Esther is a little old lady who was raised on a farm herself." Honora has come up behind me. "She isn't Amish, but their lack of materialism has an impact on her work."

There are several more stately rooms in the gallery, housing more paintings; there are sculptures displayed on tall white columns. I'm admiring *Cherry Burl Bowl. Vaughn Delaney, $900* when Honora whoops with delight.

"Hughie, my love!" she cries and throws her arms around the man who has entered the room. Hughie gently places his hands on either side of Honora's head scarf and tilts her face to his. There is a lingering kiss, and I turn my back in embarrassment.

"Andrea, this is Hughie Nye. Hughie, I'd like you to meet my new assistant, Andrea."

"An assistant, eh?" Hughie offers his hand and I shake it awkwardly. "Suddenly Nora Menapace is this elite artist, flouncing around with an assistant. So you are an artist, too, Andrea?"

I open my mouth and shoot Honora an anxious glance. She nods encouragingly, then rescues me just when I feel tears of shame spring to my eyes.

"Andrea is an artist," Nora says, taking Hughie's arm.
"She's in search of her medium."

"Ah, yes." Hughie nods. "I remember that stage."

"Hughie is a writer," Honora explains to me. "He was short-listed as poet laureate of the United States in 1984, among many other accomplishments."

"Indeed," Hughie says, clasping Honora's arm and leading her to the hallway. "I tried many different formats before I settled on poetry. I think I secretly despised poetry, and desired to write epic novels of complex plot. I managed to publish one such novel. I enjoyed it about as much as shoveling Zena's dog shit off the dahlias in my backyard when she comes to visit me."

Honora laughs.

"How is the darling dog, anyway?" Hughie asks.

"Zena is Zena," Honora says.

"Inquisitive beast, waterfall of drool," Hughie says, playfully nudging Honora's side. "Are you two spending the night with me?"

Honora shakes her head.

"Zena is alone, and I have too many things to get done."

"Indeed," Hughie says again.

Hughie leads us to the stairs. He unhooks the chain blocking the magnificent staircase and ushers us through. He hitches it closed behind us.

"Curtis is doing the books in the study," he says as we pause at the top of the staircase. "Come into the parlor."

I look down over the rail, where a bronze chandelier holds dozens of crystal lights. I imagine briefly what it would be like living here. I imagine our seedy brown sofa and soda-can-littered coffee table here, and Mom's hospital uniform hanging over the railing to dry. I imagine Ashley calling up to me from the bottom of the staircase, asking if I want to go for a ride in her Mom-i-van.

Hughie's parlor is full of antiques, polished and posed elegantly on high dark tables and inset shelves. A few of the shelves have glass covering their fronts.

"Andrea, this is a vase from the Ming Dynasty of China, circa 1400." Hughie taps the glass protecting a weathered urn with intricate designs painted on its surface.

"The colors are so vibrant," I say. I remember my near-tears downstairs and feel like a foolish girl eying nail polish in the display rack at Rite Aid.

"Aren't they?" Hughie replies. "You almost want to lick them to see what they taste like. Honora, my love, can I offer you a drink? Andrea?"

Hughie bustles off before we can answer. Honora kicks off her shoes and curls up on a small, stout couch with huge brass buttons securing its upholstery. She yawns and offers me a wan smile.

"Now you've met Hughie. A poet who resists the urge to lick centuries-old pottery and whisks away Saint Bernard puppies from undesirable parents."

Honora closes her eyes for a moment, and I notice her face looks old and drawn. Dark circles have gathered below her eyes. Her head scarf looks rumpled, as does her white linen shirt.

"Andrea, I go back to the hospital for treatment the day after tomorrow," she says. "I'm going to drive to Philadelphia tomorrow afternoon, since my appointment is first thing the next morning. Can you take care of Zena for me?"

"Of course," I answer. When we both look up, Hughie's standing there with a tray of steaming tea. He sets down his tray and kisses Honora's hand, then holds it to his cheek.

"Would you like some mint honey in your tea, darling?" he asks, his eyes welling with tears.

Mom and Dennis have joined a new couples bowling league that meets Friday nights.

They bought matching yellow bowling shirts and wear khaki pants that strain to cover their individual bulks.

"Want to come?" Dennis asks me while Mom locates her purse in the kitchen. I have a feeling his invitation is genuine, but he won't hold it against me if I say no.

"No, thanks. I have to walk the dog."

"Shame you don't have your own dog to walk," Dennis says, bending over to scratch his shins. "But I guess you wouldn't get paid so damn much to walk your own dog."

I've been keeping Honora's seventy dollars a week on my bureau, inside the raku vase she gave to me. When I lie in bed at night, I spend it on clay, a prom dress, a Jeep Cherokee. I don't know what to do with it yet, except to let it collect.

Dennis seems to be waiting for me to speak, then grunts when I don't offer any information about the job. He does it like he doesn't care either way if I tell him about it or not; it's my business after all.

I think of Ashley, how she didn't need my friendship. She didn't need to speak to me at all. And, like Dennis, she had done it anyway.

I decide to sit in the rocking chair. I look at Dennis, who

stops rubbing his shins long enough to check for grit beneath his fingernails.

I try to think of something to say.

"I think I'm going to get my driver's license."

As soon as I've said it, I wonder if it's a huge mistake. Dennis grunts again. He still doesn't look at me.

"I have to go to the motor vehicles department to get the permit application," I press on. I feel reckless, like I did that night I marched up Roger Dupris's driveway to the porch light. I'm afraid Dennis will reject me, or worse—tell Mom.

Dennis finally looks at me.

"I'll drive you over Saturday morning," he says.

"What should I tell Mom?" I ask.

"That piece is all yours to figure out. I'll just be in the driveway around ten. What you tell her is your business."

"Deal," I say.

"Hey, Andrea?"

"Yeah?"

"Your mom really does want you to be happy. You know that, right?"

I stand from the rocking chair. I want to glare at him, but I can't raise my eyes to meet his, too afraid of the fury it might bring to my face. How would I know that? Worse, how would *he* know that? Why did he bother with either Mom or me in the first place?

Mom bustles from the kitchen with her purse.

"Make sure you tape my shows for me," Mom says. Then, they're gone.

The days are long, and it's nearly nine o'clock and still light when I walk down my street to Honora's house. Roger Dupris's driveway is empty. Wendy Cartwright's obnoxious little brother is also absent, thankfully.

Zena trots directly to the kitchen when I open the back door. I'm soothed by her presence. She snuffles through a bowl of kibble and trots down the hallway to be let outside.

Spring has started to change into summer. Honora's gardens have become lush and comfortable, the plants no longer pushing forcefully through dirt, eager to be among the living. The path through the woods has grown narrow and crowded; prickers and tree branches with thick leaves brush my face as I follow Zena. The creek water, full of energy just a few short weeks ago, has become sullen and shallow.

I think about Honora, in the hospital. Sickness and pain are so well tucked away into the shadows of our world.

Zena careens down the ravine wall in the dark. I envy her. A creature of joy without the weight of Diego's shorn-off jawbone interrupting her sleep, mysterious scents filling her nostrils as she runs deer trails in the dark.

I decide to copy her. To run in the darkness down the steep ravine, without a path to guide me.

Each footstep is by instinct. I fail miserably at first, my toes faltering against the ravine wall, my fingers grasping for leverage. I close my eyes for fear of gouging them out on an outstretched tree branch. I would be a soggy clod facedown in the creek bed on the *Sunrise News*. Search and

Rescue folks would be trying to make sense of how I got there in the first place.

I twist myself to one side and try galloping down the ravine wall at a side step; then I get brave and run face-first. I ignore the branches whipping my cheeks. I just run. In no time I'm bursting through rotten tree-branch debris, huddled where the creek deposited it in the spring thaw. I fall to my knees in the water, surprised at how warm it is when it soaks through my clothes.

Zena doesn't seem the least bit surprised to find me there, kneeling on all fours in the creek in the dark. She slurps some water and then pricks her ears at the night sounds.

I wonder if humans have always been so inept at using their senses. Unable to smell the events of the forest at night. Unable to hear them, to see them.

It's the ultimate video game, playing in the woods. I think about Honora, summiting some remote Adirondack peak. I think about Daria's granddaughter, hypnotized by the lathe tool. Real euphoria.

I consider staying the night at Honora's. Zena isn't the type of dog you abandon. She needs me. I can see it in her forlorn expression.

Instead I head home.

Dennis's car is in our driveway. The house is dark. I stand there, just out of reach of the streetlight, and think about this.

I like Dennis well enough. But I'm not sure I'm ready to see him in his boxer shorts in the hallway every morning.

In the Leahy's house, a TV screen glitters from beyond half-closed blinds. A dog is barking somewhere over on Gray Street, and a car is humming softly in a driveway further down our cul-de-sac. I think about my mother, and know she'll never run face-first down a ravine wall in the moonlight.

I wonder if Mr. Diego ever did.

13 Final exams week at Simmonsville High School. Some kids become all business: focused, studious. Others become listless. The funny thing about finals week is it divides us kids down the middle regardless of affiliation. Goths, Smokers, Cheerleaders, even Nothings all become either the Serious or the Indifferent.

Chem notes and study sheets become hot commodities, and smart kids become everyone's friend. The In crowd for a fleeting moment: Dorks, Nerds, and Geniuses—most of them fall for it. They sit with the jocks for one lunch period, like it's a business meeting. The jocks need decent enough grades to stay out of summer school and on their teams. The nerds need to be Desirable.

Teena Santucci has plans involving her parent's summer house in New Jersey.

"My Mom is there, like, half the week," she explains at Ashley's locker to a pair of glistening, pony-tailed friends. "She said if I can get a job at, like, a gift shop or something, I can stay down there for July and August."

"You can't!" wails a friend. "You'll miss everything here!"

Teena shrugs petulantly and bats her eyelashes.

"Yeah, but think of the college guys working down there at the shore," she says. "We'll have to get your moms to let you come see me on a couple of weekends."

The friends contemplate this enticement, then smile

hopefully. Act 3—Teena Santucci Secures Her Popularity Status.

Ashley is among the Serious on finals week. I learn this as I watch her for a few days, frowning at notebooks in the hall and wearing baggy sweatshirts.

"Crap. I've got to get to Spanish review like ten minutes ago," she tells her friends. They drift down the hall, their voices like cheerful birds.

"Andrea?"

I smile at Ashley, who has caught her sweatshirt in the ring of a notebook binder.

"I have something kind of weird to ask you."

Ashley's smile is apologetic but genuine.

"My mom is flying home from Colorado Friday night. She's been visiting my aunt. Anyway, she won't be back until midnight, and it's prom night. Do you want to come over for a little while? You don't have to see me off, unless you want to, but I'd love some help with my nails and makeup. It just seemed more weird to get ready alone than it was to ask you if you wanted to come."

Ashley laughs awkwardly.

"My dad will be home around six, and Bryan is picking me up at six-thirty. At least he'll be there for pictures and stuff. It's my first prom."

Ashley's face turns red.

"Next year we'll both be going. It's just that Bryan's a junior." She finishes, confused. "I'm sorry. Maybe I shouldn't have asked."

There is a brief silence between us, and I can hear the

Doughnut's feet shuffle toward her door. Time to clear the hall.

"It depends," I say. "It depends on what color your dress is."

"Turquoise."

"Jewelry?"

"Rhinestones. One choker necklace and a fake tennis bracelet."

"Shoes?"

"Hideous dyed-turquoise things, like you'd wear to Teena Santucci's spaghetti-buffet wedding reception."

When we burst out laughing, the Doughnut's head comes out of her classroom.

On the bus ride home from school, Wendy Cartwright's little brother Paul victimizes an eighth grader. Wendy leaves welts in his arm where she grabs him and shoves him in a seat. We all ride the rest of the way with our faces averted.

14 Dennis has bought Mom a kitten.

Dennis is lying on our living room floor with a long piece of masking tape, sticking it loosely to the carpet in front of the kitten's face and tearing it up as its tiny claws try to grasp it. Mom's face fluctuates between annoyance and delight.

"Dennis made me get out of work early today because he had a surprise," she explains to me. "This is the surprise. This rodent."

Mom giggles, then winks at Dennis.

Dennis gets gracelessly off the floor. In his great meaty paw, he presents the kitten to me.

"This is Hefty," Dennis says. "Buddy of mine found him tied up in a plastic garbage bag next to his car repair shop."

I cringe at this, then take the tiny kitten from Dennis's outstretched hand. The kitten whirls to face me, one moment lithe, then stumbles a little at the newness of this skill.

Hefty's fur is mottled gray and black, with hints of orange. He has a pink nose and gray-blue eyes.

Mom gets off the couch and heads for the kitchen.

"I'm going to see if we have any tuna fish and milk that isn't curdled in the fridge," she says. "Otherwise, Dennis can run you down to Gimelli's for some cat food."

Dennis grins and gives me the thumbs-up. I don't smile back, but what he says next makes my heart swell.

"You have to break her in with a cat," he whispers. "Then next time, maybe it's a dog."

I study in my room with the kitten on my floor, curled up in an old bathroom towel. When he wakes up, I deposit him right into a litter box, the way Dennis told me.

Downstairs, Mom and Dennis are chatting, and I'm tempted to sneak to the top of the stairs to listen. What could Mom, or even Dennis, have to say that was so intriguing that they could talk for hours? Hefty toddles after the ball I toss. Halfway to the ball, he stops to sleep on my bedroom floor.

Tomorrow is Friday, the last day of finals. Prom night for Ashley. The day Honora comes back from Philadelphia with another round of chemotherapy coursing through her veins.

Mom laughs downstairs, and I think of all the nights there had been no laughter in our living room, except for the laugh tracks from Mom's TV shows. I force myself to stare at my math study sheet until after midnight, hoping the kitten will wake up again. When he does, I put him in the litter box, then watch him while he explores my room.

I hear the front door open downstairs, the start of a car's engine. Dennis drives slowly down our street, and I feel guilty for hoping he'll come back with a puppy sometime in the future. Sometime when Mom feels safe enough to allow a little more chaos than just a new rocking chair, a new kitten, and a few laughs. When Dennis would be a comfortable fixture in our lives. Mom needs that.

Maybe I need it, too.

15 Honora is sleeping when I arrive to let Zena out.

My exhilaration at having completed finals week fades, then fills me up again when I read a note left on the kitchen counter:

> *And And—*
> *Please walk Zena. I'm fine, just need a power nap. If you're free, come back at dark tonight. Glazing.*
> *Nora*

16 Ashley is wearing a huge terry-cloth bathrobe and dog slippers when she opens her front door.

"Beware," she says. "The fleabags are going to come busting in any second."

I've never been inside Ashley's house. I have a brief moment to look at a painting, propped on an easel in the front hall. It's of a young boy, all freckles and gap-toothed grin of innocence. Then the dogs arrive in a flurry of toenails on wood floors, greeting me.

Ashley leads me upstairs and the dogs follow us to her bedroom.

"Not tonight, babies," Ashley says, closing her door gently in their expectant faces. "I hate doing that to them."

Ashley's room is a combination of little girl and teenager decor. There's a huge vanity, mirror edge taped with photos and ticket stubs. Stuffed animals are grouped on a painted white shelf; there's an India-print bedspread with marching elephants painted like Easter eggs. There's a hamper stuffed tight with dirty clothes, and pink flowers on her eyelet curtains.

To me, the room reflects Ashley perfectly. Cheerleader with well-loved stuffed animals. Daddy's little princess with a big heart and perfect smile.

I do not begrudge her this. Ashley has accepted me with

an open mind and I've decided to try my hardest to return the favor. Especially now that I know Ashley is so much more than what I assumed she was. "Cheerleader" and "Princess" don't even begin to define her.

Ashley's closet door is partly open so that a long sequined gown can hang uninterrupted to the floor from the doorjamb. The dress has spaghetti straps. I'm slightly envious. On me, the dress would probably have an appalling, lumpy shape. On Ashley, it will be perfect.

She plops down on the bed and unwinds the towel from her damp hair. She rubs her head vigorously and wads up the towel for a toss into the laundry hamper.

"There," she says. "It'll be dry by the time my mom gets to it tomorrow morning. She spends half her life cleaning, chasing dog hair around with the vacuum cleaner. The other half, straightening my brother's portraits." She laughs.

"My mom goes to antique shows and lets her boyfriend sleep over at our house on the second date," I offer.

We both crack up.

Ashley wants me to put nail polish on her. I've never put nail polish on someone else before. I've never even put it on myself.

"Here." She thrusts the bottle at me and splays her fingers out on her kneecaps. The cap reads GOLDEN APPLE. I brush it on with timid strokes, and Ashley talks.

"So, when you go to the prom next year, who do you think you'll go with?"

I shrug. "Please. There's no guy at Simmonsville who will meet my high ugly-girl standards."

"What are you talking about? You're not ugly," Ashley says, surprised. "Don't you know anyone beautiful who doesn't look like a makeup ad model?"

Ashley waves her hands to dry my paint job. I hesitate while she inspects it.

"Yes. I guess."

Ashley nods her approval of her nails and stands up.

"You're brooding," she says. "Highly sexy if you package it right. Let your bangs grow out, wear charcoal eyeliner and black boots."

I watch Ashley pluck her already-perfect eyebrows with dainty tweezers, then she turns her back to slip off her robe. In a moment, she's pulling the turquoise gown over her thighs. Ashley is definitely makeup model beautiful. A beauty so different than Honora's.

But the one thing Ashley does share with Honora is wisdom.

It occurs to me for the first time how beautiful Honora must have been when she was young. It's there, in the way she dresses in extraordinary clothes with no self-consciousness, the way she laughs fearlessly and doesn't care about a smear of garden dirt on her face.

It's there, too, in the noble way she endured the loss of her hair to the cancer treatments. She'd lost it and never once mentioned it to me, as if the event was too trivial in her life to warrant anything more than the private selection of unusual turbans and scarves.

Honora wasn't makeup ad beautiful. She was beautiful in a more dignified way.

"That looks amazing," I say when Ashley finishes

blow-drying her short hair and latching jewelry around her neck and wrists. "Your hair, your makeup. You look like an actress at an awards show."

Ashley crosses her eyes, snorts, and scratches her armpit. We both laugh, and she cracks a joke about how shaky Bryan Davenport's hands are going to be when he pins on her corsage in front of Big Daddy.

"It's almost six-fifteen," she says. "Dad should be here by now."

Ashley's dad arrives at the same time as Ashley's prom date. There's a flurry of talk and awkward camera poses in the driveway, then she's gone. Her dad and I nod at each other. Then I ride my bike down his driveway in silence.

17 Zena and Honora are in the cobblestone shed. Zena's stretched out on the floor and Honora's stirring a vat of milky batter.

Honora's arms are purple with bruises. Her neck looks too long beneath a black winter skullcap. But her eyes are blazing with the familiar allure of the work, her smile gentle and pleased.

"White dead nettles," she says, and goes back to stirring her pot. "A tiny white flower on a green stem. The green is so rich, it draws your eyes more than the homely little flower. The more dainty cousin to the stinging nettle. White dead nettles don't sting."

I pull a stool closer to Honora's worktable and watch her. She's using a wooden spoon to stir the batter. When she finishes, she puts the spoon in a bucket of murky water.

"Looks like you're making pancakes."

Honora laughs.

"Pottery glaze. Powder plus water plus stir, and you've got your art a layer of skin. It's the form and structure of the piece, perfectly coupled with an extraordinary glaze, that gives you the final result."

Honora pours her mixture into a glass canning jar and screws the top on. She shakes it so vigorously that the bones of her arms jut out.

"The name of this glaze is White Dead Nettles. At least

193

that's what I've named it. It's essentially white, but if you look beyond the white, you see a green sheen that gradually overpowers your impression of the white. It's a delayed perception of color, and it's a wonderful sensation if you allow yourself the time it takes to experience it."

Honora hands me an ordinary paintbrush and takes my hand.

"Before you put any glaze on the brush, practice your strokes," she says. "Like this, steady and clean, no clumps or drips."

My first bowl I clump the glaze and need Honora to help me fix it. After that I glaze each piece she places at my end of the worktable in silence. Honora mixes another batch of glaze, this one the color of an aged brick building.

"What do you call that one?" I ask.

"Red Number Twenty-four," Honora answers with a smirk.

We both chuckle.

18 Sometimes, when I lie in bed, I contemplate how much more content with my life I've become. I'm satisfied with the events of a certain day, like the road trip with Honora and the day Ashley nearly backed her Mom-i-van into the ditch at the end of my driveway. I try to remember the other times in my life I've felt happy. I think of Victor Rizzo and Dad. About the holes left in my life when they went away.

I think about the Doughnut knowing my name when I thought she didn't, when Ashley confided in me at our lockers. Dennis telling me my mom wanted me to be happy. Why hadn't *she* been happy, all these years? Mom had stuck with me. She had given me a home with a parent who got a steady paycheck but had she ever given me love? Had I not deserved it, somehow?

When I get home from walking Zena and tending to an ailing Honora Sunday afternoon, Dennis is lying on our couch with his shoes off.

Mom is standing over him like a hawk in polyester pants, cracking her knuckles anxiously.

"Dennis has had a little incident," Mom reports, not taking her eyes from his pouting face. "He was in the bathroom cleaning out his ear with a cotton swab. He bent over to pick up something off the floor, and he whacked his head on the sink. It forced the swab way into his ear."

I can tell by Mom's posture she's being penitent. She'd probably met Dennis at the bathroom door and found great hilarity in his predicament, until she realized he was really hurt. Now she's making amends by babying him.

"Shouldn't you go to the emergency room?" I ask, picking up Hefty in my arms and smelling his kitten smell.

"I don't think it's punctured," Dennis whispers. "Just hurts like hell."

Mom changes the hot pack pressed to his balding, mis-shapen head. Dennis grunts in satisfaction, and Mom is pleased. When she heads to the kitchen to make him dinner, he removes the hot pack from his head and sits up on our couch so that he can reach his legs.

"Shin splints," he says, placing the hot pack on one of the offending shins. "Guess I need to take off some weight."

Dennis lowers himself back down on the couch and places the hot pack to his ear.

"I picked something up for you," he says.

I smile.

"Pop-Tarts?"

Dennis chuckles.

"Driver's permit study booklet," he says. "You'll need it for the test."

Mom's footsteps are approaching from the kitchen.

"I tossed it in your room on the dresser, if you want it," Dennis says, just before Mom comes back with a tray of potato chips and sandwiches.

I head up the stairs for my bedroom.

"Oh wait, Andrea," Mom calls. "A girl called for you. Ashley. She wants you to give her a call back."

I close my bedroom door and set Hefty on my bed. He stabs a tiny claw at my pillowcase.

I've never, not once, gotten a phone call from a friend. When Victor lived here, he just walked to my front door and pounded.

Ashley's number is in the phone book. She answers, and tells me every sordid detail of prom night.

"I broke up with Bryan. Seems he and Teena Santucci have a thing on the side. They snuck out in the hall while I was dancing with some of the cheerleaders. Everyone saw them making out. It's *so* over.

"And you should have seen what Teena was wearing. She looked like a slut Popsicle. It was like this bikini-top thing with a mermaid skirt. Unbelievable. The seniors were laughing at her."

I think about Ashley, disgraced by her boyfriend and Teena Santucci at the prom. About how I used to think she was unburdened, before she confided in me about her hair, her brother, and her distaste of popularity. Before I knew more about who Ashley really is.

It's hard to know another person. It's like everyone fades and glows in ever-changing light. Like we're each a playing card in a deck random only to a certain point, yet still

197

random enough to keep us guessing which card will be played next.

Ashley giggles into the phone.

"I've got to go," she says. "And now that you've listened to me explode—thanks for helping me get ready. At least when I got totally humiliated, I looked excellent."

19 Monday is the last day of school. We're back only as a formality now: cleaning out lockers, reading exam scores next to our student ID numbers in the hallways. There are no seniors around; they're not required to come anymore and we're left without their extraordinary presence, setting right the hierarchy of high school. Suddenly, we've moved up a notch, without having deserved a higher ranking in the world other than that the real seniors are gone.

We also have to go to the Moving Up Day ceremony, which is a ridiculous assortment of inspirational speeches and snarling admonishments. Don't drink and drive. You can be whatever you want to be in life.

"Except, apparently, you can't be a drunk driver," Ashley whispers to me. "You can be whatever *else* you want to be."

I snicker.

Ashley has been keeping her distance from Teena Santucci today. Teena seems uncomfortable when she shoots a glance our way in the school auditorium. The students are all listless: Outside there are cars full of beach blankets; a beeline to Hinckley Lake will make its way along County Route 11 as soon as school lets out. Those of us with no plans will savor the freedom from school for a moment before we set off: we'll either spend the summer hiding in a loneliness preferable to school, or we'll chase our own private dreams. This summer, I'm going to take choice two.

Principal Guthrie finishes his speech about drinking and driving, and introduces the figure making his way on-stage with an outstretched hand. Mr. Ferris.

Fag Feet Ferris is wearing his faded brown corduroys. He walks sheepishly across the stage and bends into the microphone.

"By a show of hands, how many of you think this assembly is just a cruel joke we teachers want to play on you kids?"

There's a spatter of laughter in the crowd, several raised hands. A football player in front of me half-shouts, "Get the hell off the stage!" His friends guffaw, but the small ruckus is lost in the general unrest of the entire student body, minus seniors.

"But this assembly is a serious matter, folks," Ferris continues. "We need to acknowledge your short passage here through the halls at Simmonsville High, and pause briefly to reflect on those events that have changed us this year.

"We have all grown, and learned, and found out a little bit more about ourselves," Ferris says. "It's what you take away from this year that will help you to become the person you are meant to be."

Ferris directs our attention to the exit at the side of the auditorium. There are two senior track kids, too-skinny boys headed for college in a few short months, holding a tree between them.

"Is that a frigging tree?" Ashley whispers.

"Yes, that would be a frigging tree," I reply, equally confused by the absurdity of it.

Ferris says, "The senior class has graciously donated this Bradford pear tree to Simmonsville High. It will be placed near the front entrance of the school, with a plaque memorializing Eduardo Diego for his ceaseless service to our school."

There are muffled reactions in the crowd.

"My mother thinks Diego killed himself just to harm the precious children of Simmonsville," I say to Ashley.

"What do you think?" Ashley asks. Ferris is talking again.

"I think it doesn't matter what I think," I whisper.

Then Moving Up Day is thankfully over, and we sophomores emerge from the auditorium for the last time before being cast in the roles of the junior class, a performance we will carry out in the fall.

Ashley and I part ways in my driveway, after we've removed my bike from the Mom-i-van.

"I'm going to be around all summer if you want to do stuff," Ashley offers. "I'm going to try to get a job at Dairy Queen, but other than that . . ."

"I'll be around, too." I smile.

So now I have plans with Ashley, however vague, for the summer.

20 Honora is dressed in a white Victorian nightgown with lilac lacing up the front, lying on the velvet couch in her parlor.

A white towel is wrapped turban-style around her head. There's an easel pulled up beside her, bold smears of paint on the canvas.

"I'm trying painting from a new perspective." Honora laughs weakly. "I call it lying on one's side with a barf bucket below."

"I think that if it doesn't work for you, it's something Hughie can use," I answer. Honora laughs again, then coughs.

"If you can get him to write a poem about me puking with a paintbrush in my hand, make sure he reads it at my funeral."

"You're not going to have a funeral yet, Honora," I say.

"You can't outrun the sunrise," she answers and then points at the canvas. "I'm trying to get the background right for this one. I want it to be hopeful. Lovely. Dreary. Subdued. Hard set of rules for a background."

"Have you called your son in New York yet?" I ask. "I mean, to tell him you're sick?"

Zena is lying next to Honora's puke bucket. I can see the worry in her eyes, the helpless way they urge me to solve whatever problem has beset Honora.

"Purple sage," Honora answers. "That's what I need. Can you bring me back some, when you come in from walking Zena?"

The leaf I bring back from Honora's herb garden is covered with soft hair.

"What color would you call this?" Honora asks me.

I think of the wine Mom and Gloria gave me when Diego died, the way it warmed my throat and hands, but looked so bloody in my glass.

"His Majesty's cloak, stained with red wine."

"You're getting the hang of this art thing." Honora smiles. "Set it on my canvas. That's the color I want."

She begins painting again.

At the back gate, I stop to look over the gardens. Fragile pink blossoms have given way to ruddy green leaves. A honeysuckle bush is growing strong; it looks like it will never die back in the cold of winter. Hostas and myrtle completely hide the earth below them. It looks so little like what I saw weeks ago, when I first came to face Zena. A prism, changing. Its beauty still there, but less tenacious.

21 Ashley and Roger Dupris both land summer jobs at the Dairy Queen near Simmonsville Park.

"It's not too bad," Ashley says to me, glancing in the rearview mirror of the Mom-i-van before backing down my driveway. "The uniform is kind of humiliating."

She shrugs her shoulders, like she's made peace with the Dairy Queen uniform, but the fact she loathes it won't change.

It's the second week of summer vacation, and Roger Dupris isn't in his driveway as Ashley settles back in the van seat to navigate our road. When we pass Honora's, I glance up at the fierce old house on the hill, and grin at the odd cement pool in its front yard, surrounded by wrought iron, shrubs, and weeds.

I understand now that Honora hadn't let the pool fall into disrepair through neglect. She thought it was more interesting like this, soft dark water in a bottomless pit, leaves and tree branches submerged and unseen. And I realize how strange it is, that just a few months ago, before I first met Honora, I'd thought she was an old lady who couldn't maintain her house, who had no friends to care for her. How quickly she's become my best friend. How she's taught me to open up, just enough, to let the good stuff in.

Ashley flicks on the signal at the end of our road and glides to a stop.

"I made an appointment for tomorrow to take the test for my learner's permit," I tell her.

"Excellent," Ashley says. "Driving is pretty cool." She cranks the air conditioner knob and giggles.

While waiting for a few cars to pass before turning onto County Route 11, Ashley scolds the Newfy in the back for shaking his head and letting loose a glob of drool from his jowls. The drool goes airborne and lands on the dashboard of the Mom-i-van.

"That's just disgusting, Kooky."

She shudders and giggles again. Her blonde hair is windblown, and summer has brought freckles out on her tanned cheeks.

"My dad keeps a roll of paper towels in here for incidents such as this," Ashley says. "It's somewhere by your feet."

I rustle my hand around under my seat. The paper towels are there and I tear a sheet free. I wipe the slimy mucous off the dashboard.

I pretend to gag. We both laugh.

"Zena has a circle on her head," I say. "It's almost perfectly round."

I draw a circle on the crown of my head. I feel instantly foolish.

Ashley smiles.

"I know what it's called when that happens," she says. "A monk's cap."

"A monk's cap? I think that's a kind of flower," I say.

I remember Honora describing a tiny yellow flower growing inside the folds of a cactus she had once seen in a desert she'd visited with her husband in Texas.

"Yeah, a monk's cap is a kind of flower," I say. "I'm pretty sure."

I tell her more about Honora's herbs, about the apothecary drawers in her cold pantry, labeled with all the mysterious words that sound nice when I say them out loud. Meadowsweet and agrimony and loosestrife.

"I guess it could be a flower." Ashley shrugs. "One of those words with more than one meaning, you know. But it's also a monk's cap on a dog's head. It only happens on Saint Bernards.

"It's like a legend. My dad told me and my brother stories like that at bedtime when we were little." Ashley flicks on her signal to turn left toward the park. I think about Mom, never once reading me a bedtime story, at least that I can remember.

Ashley glides through the parking lot.

"Anyway, the legend goes like this."

Ashley tells me about poor people in Europe walking over the Alps for food and jobs. If they were lucky enough not to get robbed and killed, they had to face regular rounds of avalanches and blizzards.

"So these religious monks lived nearby, and being all monklike they helped people along the path." Ashley finds a parking spot.

"The monks, they trained dogs to dig people out of avalanches and guide them back to the monk palace during snowstorms. Here's the kicker: the name of the monk palace is Saint Bernard. Ta-da."

Ashley laughs triumphantly, like she has just succeeded in remembering the punch line to a good joke and has also managed to time its delivery just right.

"What's that have to do with the spot on Zena's head?" I ask.

"That's the monk's cap," Ashley says. She points to her head. "See, the legend goes that the monks put them there as their calling card."

I consider Ashley's story and shake my head at how perfectly it suits Zena.

"Don't monks wear hoods, not caps?" I ask.

"Who the hell knows?" Ashley laughs, and I laugh too.

"It's funny how words like *monk's cap* could have so many different meanings," I say. The three dogs in the back begin shoving each other for the best position to leap free from the van. Ashley swings the door open.

"You're sure learning a lot of plant and flower stuff from Honora," Ashley comments. "That's pretty cool."

"Yeah."

Ashley releases the pack of dogs and they careen to three different patches of lawn and plant their muzzles in the earth, noses quivering. I wonder what they're finding out.

"Check it out," Ashley says. "Hot guy by the tennis courts."

I look.

"That's Keiran," I say. "He's one of Roger Dupris's driveway basketball buddies."

"He must not be on varsity yet." Ashley squints to get a better look at Keiran.

"He's a freshman, but Roger's a sophomore, like us," I say.

"Juniors, now." Ashley stops gazing at Keiran and punches my shoulder playfully. She removes a tennis ball from the pocket of her shorts.

"Come on, stupids!" she hollers. "Fetch!"

All three dogs run for the tennis ball Ashley throws. The Newfy lumbers along good-naturedly without any real desire to reach it first, the Labs are more fierce in their competition for the rights to wield the ball and return it to Ashley's outstretched hand.

She hands me the ball to take a few turns.

I throw.

"Ashley, Honora is really sick," I say.

Until now, I have shared this secret with no one.

Ashley wipes a patch of dog slobber from the front of her shorts, frowning.

"Is she in major pain?" she asks.

"She wouldn't tell me if she was," I say, then think about it for a few seconds. "Not really, she wouldn't."

"Does she moan?"

"No."

Ashley weighs this. She shakes her head slowly, as though rendering a diagnosis requires her to travel to her own painful place.

She sighs.

"When my brother was sick—when he was dying—he moaned a lot. The pain got excruciating. It sounded like there were invisible steel clamps or something crushing his head. Eventually, he just gave out."

"Oh."

I look at Ashley, at her calm sorrow that must have once been heartbreaking, but has now faded to acceptance. Her brother was dead. And she was well into the process of moving on with her life, with a different pace and more wisdom than she had had during his life.

Ashley's hair is no longer a bad haircut; a slight sheen of sweat from the summer sun has made her bangs curly. She gives me a wide smile.

"My aunt is coming to visit us from Colorado. At least that'll keep my mom busy for a week."

I laugh.

"They're going to box up my brother's things. Donate some stuff to the thrift shop downtown, save others for keepsakes. His room's going to become a spare bedroom. Instead of a shrine."

I hand the tennis ball back to Ashley.

I think about the old recliner that Dennis replaced with my mother's new antique rocker in our living room. About his bowling nights with Mom in her too-tight bowling pants; about the kitten he had plunked down on our living room carpet, the one that curled up on Mom's bathrobe at night while she caught up on her TV sitcoms.

Little changes that had perked Mom up and given her companionship. Each provided by Dennis. Dennis had brought her a sense of security that I had never been able to provide; Mom had been too worried making sure her vigil over my life never faltered.

She had never enjoyed a minute of it.

I wondered if Ashley's mother had enjoyed her time with her son, or had she spent it vacuuming? Ashley had loved her brother enough to know that after a few years, the best gift she could give him was to let him become a legend.

"I think dogs know things we'll never know," Ashley says, sliding back the door of the Mom-i-van and letting the dogs jump inside. Keiran is no longer on the tennis courts. Ashley climbs back into the driver's seat, slams her door, and blasts the air conditioner.

"I have to go get ready for work," she sighs.

We drive home in companionable silence.

When Ashley drops me off in my driveway, Dennis is just leaving. I look away when he plants a kiss on Mom's cheek at the door.

"Tomorrow at ten, driver's permit test," I whisper as he passes me in the driveway.

"I'll drive you over," he says, winking.

22 I keep my driver's permit in the glove box of Dennis's car.

My first lesson, I drive with my hands so tight on the steering wheel, my knuckles bulge. Neighborhood houses slide past the car windows, the painted lines of our cul-de-sac carve the route I am meant to follow. I am totally alert—even though the car is only going about three miles an hour.

"Give it a little gas," Dennis says. "That's it. Now, train your mind to follow the road."

We drive with no destination. At each intersection, I hold my foot against the brake fiercely while we reason out the steps I'm meant to take. Put on the turn signal. Look both ways. Be aware of your surroundings.

And drive.

I love driving.

Dennis rolls down his window and sticks his elbow out. The sudden blast of wind drowns out the screeching voice of some eighties arena rock star penetrating from the duct-taped stereo speakers. Dennis is wearing an adventurous grin, and soon the steering wheel in my hands and the pedals at my feet find a rhythm that feels right, just enough to attempt a three-point turn on the uncertain asphalt somewhere outside Simmonsville, on a road not many people use. Once, a deer darts into the road and Dennis slams his

211

cross trainers down on the floor of the passenger side, using his own invisible brakes.

"Shit." His voice cracks. I calmly slow down and veer in a gentle swoop, checking for other cars. Both deer and car make a clean getaway. I think of Amelia Earhart.

"I think I'd like to fly a plane someday," I say to Dennis, who is checking his seat belt.

Dennis waits a moment before chuckling, more to himself than to me.

"You're the type of kid who just might, Andrea," he says.

I think I hear the slightest hint of respect in his voice.

23 Ever since school let out, I head to Honora's around ten each morning. I learn to mix glazes on my own, and we eat weightless salads from her garden, flavored with crusty-herb vinegar oil and washed down with organic blueberry juice.

Honora is growing thinner every day. Her arms are bonier and her summer peasant dresses hang awkwardly on her shoulders. Her eyes, however, are still vivid. Her smile is still unapologetic. At times it can almost make me forget what the other stuff means. How sick she is.

Today, Honora is writing her will.

She has a spiral-bound notebook on her knees and wool socks on her feet. Her turban looks like an Indian sari printed with lotus flowers; it's tied in a knot on top of her head.

"You look like a snake charmer," I say.

"Fabulous to be a snake charmer for a day, wouldn't it?" Honora says. "This is Sri Lankan." She touches her headpiece.

Zena nudges my knee for her walk and I head for the door. She follows, dancing in anticipation.

"I have an appointment for my driver's test Wednesday," I say. "I'm really excited."

"Doesn't it feel good to be passionate?" Honora grins. "And such ideal timing. I'm feeling a little too weak these

213

past few days to be driving. I should be done with this by then." Honora's wrist trembles slightly when she holds up the stack of handwritten notes on elegant stationery. I think of her scrawly handwriting, written words that captured her unusual perspective on life.

"I'm being painfully specific, a little joke I'll play on Hughie." Honora chuckles. "He's the executor, the person who agreed to carry out my final wishes. I think he'll find great humor in attending to some of them. They're pretty entertaining, in a subtle way.

"Anyway, when you get your license you can drive me down to the lawyer's office to file this," Honora says.

"Such enticement for me to pass the test," I answer. I notice, ashamed, that my voice is quavery.

Honora puts down her pen and walks over to me. She places her hands firmly on my cheeks.

"Andrea, we are two people at very different times in our lives," she says. "There's a reason you were led to me, and I to you. But you must understand that we are on different paths, you and I. We've met by chance at the crossroads."

I'm suddenly angry. I'm enraged at her, for trapping me in her web of need, like I was the Geek with all the answers the night before final exams.

"Andrea, you need to know," Honora continues. "There's nothing left between me and death now but my own ability to heal myself. There's nothing left that doctors can do, or intravenous drugs, or even more surgery.

"It's down to the ninth inning, and I've got an out or

two left. And based on my white blood count, it seems the score is heavily in the opponent's favor."

"People get cured of cancer all the time!" I scream at her. "You need to get a new doctor, go to a bigger city!" My tears are like hot welts on my cheeks, my lips sting with salt. I'm shocked by my reaction—my fury.

"I guess I think differently than most folks," Honora says. "I think the reason the world is a mystical, enchanting place, is because of the cycle of life. My body will decompose, but maybe some little element of it will be transformed into a particle of dirt, over years and years, and then a glorious flower will be nurtured by this particle of dirt. Then this flower will nourish a random bumblebee, who in turn will be eaten by a raven. So, in some future life, I'll be able to fly. I look forward to that. I've always admired the freedom of birds."

The startling purity of Honora's plan silences my sobs. I feel an infusion of wisdom.

"I'm afraid that when I die, I'll become a particle of dirt, then get swallowed by an earthworm," I say. "Then I'll be crapped out in some cavern of a massive maze. And I'll be stuck there, wishing I knew which type of creatures ate worm crap."

Honora and I both laugh.

"How do you know if death is going to be good or not?" I say.

"Doesn't matter if you think it's going to be good or not," she says simply, dropping her hands from my cheeks. "You go there, either way. You must be brave."

215

"Maybe the bravest get to fly," I answer, picking up Zena's leash. "The timid get lost in an earthworm tunnel for eternity."

Honora looks amused.

"Perhaps," she says.

Honora is putting on her boots to join Zena and me for a walk. Zena is almost incredulous with joy.

Honora walks hunched and slow. She pauses at the garden gate to stretch her back and shake out her neck. I look at her, standing there in wool socks and hiking boots, a gauzy sack dress and Sri Lankan scarf wrapped around her shrunken head. She has a hemp satchel slung on a long string around her neck. Her teeth look too big when she smiles at me, her eyeballs have a yellow tinge.

But her eyes also tell me she's still fighting this thing, testing it to see if it's just a scene in her life, or if it's the final act. She gathers some yarrow leaves in her hand and rubs her palms together fast.

"This releases their power," she explains. "Then you breathe it in."

I copy Honora and rub some of the yarrow in my palms. I take a huge whiff.

"What does it smell like?" Honora is grinning, bringing her face back down for another gasp of crushed yarrow.

"Vicks Vapo-Rub," I answer.

"Yes," answers Honora. "The scent only lasts for a moment. Mine's starting to fade a little."

She rubs again, lowering her face.

The scent isn't dreary like Vapo-Rub, though. It's

euphoric, and I keep breathing it in until it's completely gone.

Honora tosses her yarrow leaves into the bushes and begins walking with as much dignity as her failing body will allow.

"You know, aboriginal North Americans stuffed yarrow in their nostrils when they were sick. They changed it out periodically, like a Band-Aid. It's said that its potency helps clear respiratory channels in your nose, throat, and lungs. Then your blood pumps more easily, and that helps you get better. Amazing, isn't it?"

Zena is being more companionable than usual in the woods. She rests at Honora's side, instead of trotting off to investigate rotting tree husks and fox holes.

At the resting rock, Honora's perch above the creek, Honora asks me about Dennis, and then about Ashley. I keep scanning the far ravine wall, hoping to see the pert faces of baby coyotes.

"You won't see her, not here at least." Honora is also scanning the ravine wall, daring it to prove her wrong. "Once the babies are old enough to move, that's exactly what she'll do. Every creature applies its own set of logic to survival, and she's using the set of skills she has to survive. Her skills tell her she can smell the scent of birth and so will her enemies."

"Where would she be likely to move them?" I asked, still hoping they might appear.

"Oh, she keeps a map in her head, of places she associates with safety and food, and she'll pick one of them for a while. Then she'll pick another. Then her children will go do the same."

"I hope they all live," I say. Then I'm ashamed by my words.

"They may, or they may not." Honora doesn't seem to notice my cruel choice of hope. Like by wishing for the lives of the babies, I'd be sacrificing any hope to win a miracle for Honora instead. Honora doesn't think this way.

"Randomness is mysterious. But it keeps us interested. It keeps us hoping."

"Do you think Zena hopes? I mean, knows what it feels like to really hope for something?"

"Yes," Honora says. "But I think the thing I admire most about Zena is that she possesses something that eludes most humans. Contentment."

"Contentment?"

"Yes," Honora says. "To be content is such a wonderful thing, isn't it?"

We walk. When we get back to the porch, Honora is exhausted.

"Tea, then a power nap," she announces, more for herself than me. "Andrea, could you boil me some nettles and chamomile?"

When I bring the steaming tea in to Honora, she's lying on her sofa, her mouth ajar. She breathes evenly, and I don't wake her up.

The next day, I tell Mom about the driving, so Dennis won't have to.

Mom is catching up on her sitcoms when I mention it, casually. Just a couple of short trips around the neighborhood. I wanted to try it out before I decided if I really wanted to pursue it. Then I had planned to surprise her by driving her somewhere. Not any of this is untrue, it's all a version of reality.

"Where the hell are you going to drive?" Mom sputters. She pauses the videotape haughtily and fixes me with her stare.

"Nowhere," I say. "Maybe Honora's van to take her to the store."

"You think a reasonable woman is going to let you drive her van without having you on her insurance?" Mom snaps. "How sick is she, that she needs a nervous sixteen-year-old to cart her around town?"

I tell Mom then, in a gush of tears, about the cancer. I feel humiliated for allowing the tears to spill over my cheeks in a blubbering mush.

Mom frowns. Then I see her face slowly register surprise, and I wonder if she is surprised at the sight of her daughter sobbing. I rush upstairs, bury my face in my pillow, and ignore the kitten that is stepping on my hair.

I ride my bike to the Dairy Queen at eight-thirty.

It's not a baseball game night, so Ashley hangs over the front counter and chats with me.

"I dropped a dollop of black raspberry on my boob," Ashley says. "Not as bad as when I got a huge wad of bubble gum smeared across my butt sitting in the gym bleachers. I had to do the final cheer with a pink streak on my white polyester miniskirt. I almost dropped Teena Santucci on her head."

Behind Ashley, Roger Dupris snickers. He's stacking plastic drinking straws in a dispenser.

"She stopped by here earlier with a gaggle of Cheerleaders." Ashley drops her voice to a conspiratorial whisper. "They all acted like they didn't even know me."

I measure Ashley's expression for frustration or hurt. The girls with whom she had invested her social career had discarded her like a Dairy Queen drink cup in the trash can. Instead, I see amusement. Ashley may have lost her status, but she hasn't lost her pride.

"Apparently, I shouldn't have gotten a haircut." She laughs. "Oh, and I probably shouldn't have called Teena out as a boyfriend thief and taken a bad-uniform job at Dairy Queen, either."

I shake my head, more at Ashley's fearlessness and strength in the face of social collapse.

"Ladies and gentlemen, I've been demoted," Ashley announces, even though there is no one at the Dairy Queen except Roger Dupris and me. Roger snickers again and comes over to pat Ashley's shoulder compassionately.

"You'll hardly miss them," he says. "Really."

I smile at them, then wink at Ashley.

"You'll just have to lower your standards," I tease her.

"Oh?" Ashley wrinkles her perfect nose at me. All this time, I thought I was raising my standards."

We laugh. I feel wonderful, because this girl whom I met over nothing more than the circumstance of a bad haircut was truly my friend.

"Anyway, I can't do anything tonight," Ashley says. I fight down my disappointment. I was hoping for a joyride in her Mom-i-van, to tell her about my driving test.

"Keiran Fleet asked me to a movie." Ashley looks pleased.

"That's great," I say, but I'm not sure if I mean it.

"Before you go, I've got something for you," Ashley says. "Hope this doesn't sound too weird, but when we were going through my brother's stuff, I came across something and thought of you."

Ashley leaves the ice cream window and gets her backpack out from under the cash register. She paws through the pockets.

"Here it is," she says, returning. "My brother collected these things, but I never saw this one."

I reach out my palm to meet hers, and she drops a large marble in it.

"He kept the special ones in a cigar box. If I touched it, I got punched. He never played with those. This was in there."

The marble is translucent, pale ivory. It feels soft and cool in my hand.

"Thanks," I say.

"Look at it, close," urges Ashley. "You have to squint right down on it."

I place the marble close to my eye. Inside, frozen and silent, is the minuscule petal of a yellow flower, caught in the fleeting perfection of healthy bloom. Inscribed in tiny, golden script are the words YELLOW WILD INDIGO.

I gasp. I don't want Ashley to see my surprise, but I sense she already knows how awed I am.

"Just like that day in the park, remember? Yellow wild indigo. Bizarre coincidence."

Roger is checking the cuffs on his Dairy Queen shirt.

I clasp the marble to my chest and smile at Ashley.

When I get home, I place the marble on my plastic bedside table and lie in bed, facing it. When Hefty tries to approach this new, mysterious object, I scoop him up and hug him to my cheek.

The marble amazes me for a few hours. Then I fall asleep.

26 I pass my driver's test with flying colors.

At least that's how Dennis describes it, while I grin stupidly and hold up my brand-new temporary driver's license. Mom is standing next to our sofa with her arms folded, her sitcom tape on pause. She looks first at me, then at big dopey Dennis. I'm pretty sure we look like two Stooges, waiting to get approval from the third.

The third gives in when Dennis offers to buy us all dinner to celebrate, but only if I drive. Mom says she needs to change out of her hospital uniform first. Dennis and I do an absurd victory dance when she leaves the room. I burst out laughing, and Dennis shushes me. I notice he's trying to hold in laughter, too.

Mom lets me pick the restaurant, between Pizza Mia and Chinatown All-You-Can-Eat Buffet. Dennis chortles with approval when I choose the all-you-can-eat.

"Crab legs and butter, here I come," he says as we wait in line to get inside. Mom knocks him in the ribs with her elbow.

Chinatown Buffet is packed with half-open mouths and monster appetites, all making sure to eat more than they paid for. Mom and Dennis sit side by side in the booth, and I notice Mom's gained weight.

"Andrea, Dennis and I have been talking. We want to clue you in on the conversation."

223

Dennis shifts his haunches on the plastic booth seat to a more comfortable position. He swipes his mouth with a napkin. I twirl a chicken wing in blue-cheese sauce.

"We're talking about sharing a house together, the three of us."

In the awkward silence that follows, I think of Dad. I think about him leaving me, never looking back. Never coming back. I thought of his only lesson to me, the one about people being all different in appearances, diverse in thought. How boring life would be if things were perfectly logical and organized.

"It can be like we're housemates, or it can be like we're a family," Dennis says, gnawing gently on a sparerib. "It's up to you, Andrea."

"Okay," I answer. "It's okay."

Mom beams at Dennis, who gives me a serious nod, then a wink.

"It seems the dessert line is next, then," he says.

At Gimelli's Shop and Run, I'm cornered by Gloria.

"Oh, Andrea." She clutches my arm as if I might float right past her if she didn't anchor me in some way. Her other hand is clutching a package of No-Nonsense pantyhose with equal fervor.

"How's your mom? We just haven't had a chance to connect, tell her I miss her, okay, honey?" Gloria says in a rush.

Mr. Gimelli hands me my bone marrow package and nods at the box of kitten kibble in my basket.

"You got a menagerie over to your house, that's a good thing for a kid. Teach responsibility, my boys and girls always had them a little parakeet."

Mrs. Gimelli hollers over from the cash register.

"Thing squawked until someone say to us, 'You throw a towel over the cage.' So we throw a towel over the cage. Shut the thing right up. Some days, I don't take down the towel so the darn thing stays shut up."

I can't hide my horror. Mr. Gimelli laughs. "Don't you worry about them parakeets, Onndrea. My kids, they get the towel off, they play with the creature, they feed it and water it good. She don't know a thing."

I smile at Mr. Gimelli. I think of his teasing kindness to

Victor and me as we chose treats from his battered candy display boxes by the cash register; his gifts of bone marrow for the dog he has helped me to befriend.

I wasn't just Victor's shy friend. Mr. Gimelli knew my name after all.

He probably always had.

"Thanks, Mr. Gimelli," I say. "For everything."

I pay for my groceries and head home.

I want to be at Honora's by one o'clock.

Tonight, we raku.

28 When I tell Honora about my driver's license, she shrieks with delight.

For a moment, I glimpse the healthy Honora. She gets some cold lemon tea and pound cake from the kitchen to celebrate.

It's a hot afternoon. Honora gives Zena an ice cube to crunch. It falls out of her jowls into the dirt, but Zena is unperturbed by the coating of filth on the ice cube's surface. Dirt clings to her frothy lips and she fixes me with a thoughtful stare.

"So, will you drive me to the lawyer's today or tomorrow?" Honora asks.

"It is that . . . close? I mean, not the lawyer's office, but the reason you want to go there?"

Honora laughs so big I see the fillings in her back teeth, which have grown huge in her shrunken face.

"That's the mystery of it all." Honora shrugs. "Maybe we'll be laughing in three years that I was so anxious to file my will. Maybe we won't."

"What are the jokes in it, the things for Hughie?" I ask.

Honora stretches and smirks.

"Oh, just little things. Hughie despises tedious tasks, so I've given him a variety of those. I've put in a donation check to the hospital, with specific instructions it must be dropped off and not mailed. Hughie will hate that. He makes everyone riding in his car roll up the windows when he passes a hospital, so no germs fly in.

"Plus, he'll be making a little trip to Daria's; and he'll have to be here to let in the Ladies' Support Circle of the local abused women's shelter. I've arranged for them to hold an auction here for all my furniture and other useless belongings. Proceeds, of course, to go to the shelter. Hughie will flutter around like a bird trapped in a funeral parlor. But it will do him good."

I hesitate to ask, but Honora's being so blunt and honest, I do it.

"What about your son? Why isn't he going to be the executor?"

Honora rubs Zena's ear between her fingertips. They are both languid today. Zena shows no interest in leaving Honora's side to snuffle along the deer paths in the woods.

"My son. He's a whole story, but a separate one from my own." Honora curls her legs beneath her on the velvet sofa. Even though it's hot, she pulls a cream-colored wool afghan over her feet.

"My son is named Ian. He and I met briefly at birth, then not again until he was twenty-two. He's a wonderful young man, a credit to his parents."

"I don't understand," I say.

"I gave Ian up for adoption," Honora says. "Only he wasn't named Ian then, I called him Jay. Short for Jayhawk, to give him strength to fly."

I ease myself down on the sofa next to Honora. I'm curious, but I'm also anxious because I'm almost certain to say the wrong thing.

"Wow" is the best I can muster.

"I was seventeen years old, and the most harmful thing I could have done to him was keep him. I knew that fully, so I have never regretted it. Especially when I met him again. Since we met, I haven't spoken to him more often than a friendly card here and there, nothing obtrusive. The same has come back, and once a phone call to tell me his daughter had been born. That's it. And I know that's good."

"How could that be good? You have a family out there, a grandchild," I say. I hope my voice sounds only curious, not judgmental.

"I was at a crossroads with an opportunity to help my own baby and to help a childless couple. I was a senior in high school on my way to Dartmouth. My parents had scrimped and saved my entire life to pay for college. I could have left six lives unfulfilled, or I could fulfill them all. It was simple, really."

"Do you think he ever felt abandoned?"

"Perhaps." Honora yawns. "Most likely, until he was an adult. But then, adults know something. They know life is complicated.

"It's an interesting thing, when adopted children find their parents. Rarely is it to forge a relationship with them. It's mostly a curiosity about themselves. And that's what it was for Ian. And that's how I know he's happy and well. What a gift he gave me, telling me that."

I consider this.

Honora's son, set free to meet his destiny. A flight through time and space that led him away from her. I think of Dad, and wonder if he had thought the same thing, that

Mom and I needed to be released to fly. I think about how life sometimes ravels together in strange ways, and blame and fear and anger can be used by those who didn't see all the hues in the palette, who didn't look up from beneath the underside of a tulip, who didn't scrub free the sooty surface to reveal streaks of emerald and bronze.

Maybe I needed to let Dad go, too.

Honora yawns.

"I was married for a few years in my late twenties, but never got pregnant again. I'm not sure what kind of mother I would have made anyway, being so self-possessed and gallivanting by nature."

I try to imagine Honora, pregnant at seventeen, married in her twenties, an artist and world traveler in her thirties. It surprises me, that she was unsettled in her earlier life. I thought she had always been content. As I saw her now.

"I'll take you to the lawyer's in the morning," I say. Then I leave, so she won't see the tears in my eyes.

ACT

5

Honora dies three days after I take her to the lawyer's office.

I find her in bed. There are a bottle of morphine pills, a notebook, and a glass of water on the bedside table. I look longer at the half-full water glass than I do at Honora. I'm reluctant to take my eyes off the glass. I'll be forced to do something that requires admitting Honora is dead. Like call 911. Or console Zena. Which to do first? Both options terrify me. So I stare at the water glass as long as I can stand it.

I have always imagined a dead person's face to be peaceful. Like a Sleeping Beauty, with just a hint of wonder evident in the eyes and around the lips. Finally knowing what it is to be dead. To have an answer, however different than what we, the living, have always imagined it to be.

But Honora's face is not serene. It's puffy. Her tongue, jutted out between her jack-o'-lantern teeth. Her eyes, open and glazed. They aren't the lively eyes I knew.

They might as well be toenails.

I don't recognize the voice at first. It starts out in a growl and changes randomly to a shriek, then a growl again, followed by a helpless blabbering. It is inhuman and anguished and everywhere.

It's my own wail.

Zena places her shoulder against me until the outburst ends.

233

I call 911, then Hughie.

Zena and I wait on the front porch. I stand and watch them come, pulsing red lights and the chilling wail of sirens: the emergency rescue team dispatched to the scene. Zena stays beside me as I take them up to Honora.

Instead of staying upstairs, I take Zena to the parlor and sit on the plush velvet sofa. I stroke Zena's ears, and look around at Honora's things. The desk's litter of mail and lists, their contents forever incomplete. The last painting she had begun and never finished, with the leaf of purple sage I had delivered dried up on the easel's ledge.

One emergency team worker breaks free from the huddle around Honora and comes downstairs to sit with me. She's holding a clipboard of papers. Then the police come and we go back outside onto the porch, and even Wendy Cartwright is standing in her driveway, shielding her eyes to gaze at the old house up on the hill where the crazy lady lived.

Hughie arrives two hours later, with a man I don't recognize. He gathers me up from Honora's velvet sofa and bear-hugs me.

"Andrea, Honora's chosen one," he introduces me to the stranger. "This is Curtis."

Curtis nods solemnly at me and caresses Zena's ears. Zena's been confused and anxious since Honora was taken away in the ambulance. Sirens silent.

Hughie bustles around Honora's living room, more to keep himself busy than to accomplish anything.

"Tell me she went peacefully, Andrea," Hughie says, his fingertips brushing over Honora's easel.

I think about the glass of water on Honora's bedside table. I remember Honora's wish, when we talked about death. I try to think of the right word, the words that would give Hughie peace, give us all peace.

"I think . . . ," I begin. My throat tightens with anguish. But I'm able to fight it down, to look into Hughie's eyes, at the tears collected on the stalks of his eyelashes.

I feel the tears collecting in my own eyes.

"I think she died a content woman," I say.

"A content woman," Hughie repeats, pondering this. Then he smacks his lips.

"I can imagine a death no less perfect for her," he says, and smiles at me. "Thank you."

Then Hughie's cheeks are streaked with tears. He makes no effort to conceal them. I consider for a moment adults who treat children like they're adults, too. Like there is no difference in wisdom. Hughie is one of those adults, and I'm thankful.

Curtis and I make tea in the kitchen while Hughie reads the notebook I found next to Honora's bed. We don't speak, but we're oddly comfortable, alone in our thoughts and consoled by the presence of each other.

When Mom bursts in fifteen minutes later, the silent memorial for Honora is shattered.

"Andrea, for chrissakes," she sputters at me, leaving the back door wide open. "Why are you hanging out in a dead woman's house with her family? It's time to come home. You need to leave these people alone."

Mom is defiant. Her legs are set wide apart and her palms are on her hips. She's wearing a bowling tournament

T-shirt and polyester shorts. Her hair looks like she just got sprayed with a hose.

Curtis and Hughie seem unruffled by this crass woman in Honora's space, in our space. Hughie hops up from the sofa and faces Mom down in a way I've never seen Mom faced down. He does it with gentle expertise.

"Andrea's mom." His smile is genuine, like he approves of this bearish woman. "You have it wrong, my dear. Andrea belongs here, and you are welcome, too."

Mom looks confused, disoriented, and allows Hughie to lead her further inside and deposit a mug of tea in her fist. Mom looks down into the mug suspiciously. She eyes Hughie, then Curtis, and finally me.

"Please have a seat," Hughie says. "You have a lovely daughter. She has been a great solace to Honora in her final days. Truly spectacular. Indeed."

I wonder if Mom has used the word *indeed* in any sentence she has ever uttered. Now she looks truly confounded. I have never seen Mom look uncertain about herself, not once. She gazes around the room as if searching for the right thing to say back to Hughie.

"Thank you, but she really shouldn't be bothering you people anymore. Mrs. Menapace doesn't need to pay her for this last week of work."

"Whoa, check out the antiques in this place." Dennis, who I know now is so much more than the Clydesdale, appears in the doorway. He is huge there, loitering, waiting for an invitation, his shoulders humped a little as if from the weight of his belly. Nobody answers him at first, and he uses the opportunity to study each of us in turn. He gazes longest at me, and I feel my own eyes begging for help. Dennis winks.

"My sincerest apologies at your loss," he says grandly. Then he is inside the door, guiding Mom away. "We only stopped by to see if Andrea was all right, and if you all needed anything."

My face floods with the sincerest of gratitude for Dennis. He wanted to save me. He was not going to allow her to cut short my mourning—to invalidate my broken heart.

"Andrea can stay as long as you need her. Right, honey?" he asks Mom, who is glaring at no one in particular. She seems almost relieved to have Dennis take over. "I can imagine attending to the arrangements might take you well into the night, and if Andrea can be of any help to you, then it's okay with us."

Mom doesn't look back as Dennis whisks her out.

"Andrea, be sure to let us know the funeral arrangements so we can send flowers," Dennis calls back over his shoulder. Then they're gone, and silence fills the room.

"Don't feel dishonored, Andrea," Hughie offers kindly. "My mother once announced to a room of her conservative friends that I was a gay man—did that ever bring the dinner party to a screech of a stop. And I had to sit there for the rest of it, enduring hateful and pitying stares from a bunch of old biddies I'd known since I was five, while my mother played out this drama queen role of wronged Christian in a chiffon tea dress."

I laugh, a little. Curtis joins in.

"But, I did learn something from my mother," Hughie

says. "Fabulous taste in garments. And you have learned something important from your mother, too. Fierce determination."

I consider this for a moment, to decide if I will refute it. "I just wish she knew when she went over the top—just took it too far," I answer. "I admire determination, but not when it's coming at you like a shark."

"Yes." Hughie nods. "You seek *graceful* determination. A much more potent version indeed. It will take you far. And you have learned it from your mother."

I want to tell Hughie about my mother's brand of determination, her determination to absorb every stupid TV show and illogical romance novel ever made. Her determination to alienate her only reminder of my deadbeat father—me. But I say nothing.

Hughie saw another type of determination: that of a mother, resolutely raising a child on her own.

I ponder this one gift from Mom.

Had I absorbed it, or had I only hated it?

2 The next morning, Honora's will is to be read at the lawyer's office.

Curtis and Hughie have made no sound from Honora's guest rooms. I sit on the velvet sofa in Honora's parlor, stroking Zena's monk's cap. I think about the first time I touched Zena, her patient acceptance of my timid fingertips on that odd brown spot on her forehead. Zena had led me here. She had guided me on this path; her monk's cap the calling card of her honorable ancestors.

The front doorbell rings.

I pray it's not Mom. But I remind myself she would never knock on a dead woman's door. The dead thing made it socially acceptable to just throw the door open and walk right in.

It's not Mom. It's a florist.

James from Pocono Mountain Art has sent a massive clot of weeds in a wooden bowl to the house. There's a note attached:

In memory of a dear friend, Honora Menapace.

"The sender asked for those," the florist says, shrugging. "They're your basic forest weeds. A couple of cattails, just for depth."

I grin when I realize the florist is apologetic not about

Honora's death, but about the strangeness of James's floral arrangement.

As I'm looking for a place to set the arrangement in Honora's parlor, the phone rings.

I decide to answer it, even though it's not my phone. Who else would?

Daria is on the other end.

"Oh good, it's you, Andrea," she says when she hears my hesitant hello. She needs to be at Honora's for the wake and funeral, she explains, but is too old to drive. Have I gotten my license yet? Could I come get her?

"Of course," I reply.

"Come this afternoon," Daria says. "I'll be ready."

Curtis offers to let me drive his Chrysler to pick up Daria. I shake my head.

"I'm comfortable driving Honora's van," I say. "Can I do that?"

"Who's going to stop you?" Hughie giggles.

Hughie and Curtis insist I go with them to the lawyer's office first. When Curtis drives away from Honora's house, I see Roger Dupris watch us thoughtfully from his driveway, then wave. I can read his lips even though I can't hear his words through the car window.

Hi, Andrea.

I wave back, and it's now that I cry. Until now, I've only wailed in private. Now I allow silent tears to slide down my cheeks and collect on the front of my shirt.

I think of Honora, her hands holding my reluctant face as she stood in her kitchen with cardboard slippers on her

feet. Honora, saying my name, never finding me uninter-
esting, like I had always thought myself to be.

Andrea Anderson, you are this and so much more.

Hughie settles on some music that sounds at first like a
woman chortling in angry hopelessness. It's opera. It slowly
becomes beautiful.

3 Honora has put me in her will.

To me, she has left me the most precious of all her owned things.

Zena.

I barely hear the clauses in Honora's will that prescribe Hughie to take Zena if I cannot and place her appropriately, given that I am a minor and there has been no parental agreement for such an arrangement. Zena is mine. More, Honora has chosen the path she thought was best for Zena, and that path is to belong to Andrea Anderson. Boring, plainish me.

"Surely you're not surprised?" Hughie says on the car ride back to Honora's. He is peeved but amused by Honora's list of tasks for him. "You can't be surprised that you are Zena's, and Zena is yours."

Zena is waiting for us in her silent home. I hug her with an intensity that I'm afraid she won't tolerate, but she slurps my cheek with her tongue and Curtis laughs.

Curtis has unfurled his personality in small pieces to me. Usually quiet people make me nervous, like they're hiding an opinion of me. Curtis, however, is gentle and kind.

I hug Zena and listen to Hughie's affectionate chatter about Honora, watch Curtis's slow smile of appreciation.

"She is a brat," Hughie proclaims of Honora, fanning his face with the lawyer's paper listing his duties. "What a conniving little brat. Andrea, when you pick up Daria today, would you please have her bring that head protector thing she wears so I can use it at the damn hospital? The nerve of that woman."

Hughie lifts a set of reading glasses to his nose from where they've been resting on his chest. "She has me delivering all of her funky herbs and potions to Daria. Have you two seen how many damn shelves and drawers of dried fungus that woman kept? I'll probably end up with skin rot or warts."

Curtis starts chuckling. Hughie snorts in disdain and grins. There is sadness in his eyes.

"I will sorely miss our Honora," he says.

4 The route to Daria's house is easy to remember. As I drive I try to think of a way to get Mom to let me keep Zena. I decide that I'll fight her with every ounce of my strength if I'm denied this. With Mom, it's best to have a plan. She can play target practice with the best of ideas or intentions, but she isn't going to deny me Zena.

Dennis will be my ally. This is a huge advantage, to have Dennis in my corner. I decide I'll tell Dennis first, and see if he has any advice. I dream of running away from home if Mom says no. I could steal Honora's van, now slated for donation to the Simmonsville Meals on Wheels program. But I know that an ordinary sixteen-year-old would suddenly become a beacon when driving a stolen car with a two-hundred-pound beast in the passenger seat. I eventually would be returned, and Zena would be taken from me.

Daria is wearing a black dress with a matching head scarf. I feel the pang of my own longing for Honora. If it had been Honora waiting on the front porch with a carpet-bag and black dress, I would have told her she looked like a Russian refugee. She would have laughed and told a story about Russian refugees. But Daria isn't Honora, so I carry her bag to the van and wait for her to deposit herself on the high front seat.

"Here, eat one of these." Daria offers a palm with a gooey dark blob in it. I shudder.

"It's regular old fudge," Daria laughs. "Chocolate pecan. Amish-made."

The fudge is rich in my mouth, and I savor it.

"My mother made the most outlandish pastries when I was a kid. My brothers and I would wrinkle our faces whenever she got busy in the kitchen, knowing we'd soon be given a prune-and-nut something, fresh out of the oven. God help us.

"Whenever any one of us got a little money we could spare, we walked down to the confectioner's shop and bought fudge. We'd sit on a curb and divide it up even. Every one of us would be silent, nursing on our hunks of fudge."

Daria shifts in her seat. She's silent while she studies a cow pasture passing her window.

"I'm the only one left, all my brothers have died. I still think of the fudge. You drive very well for a young girl."

In addition to her small bag of clothes, Daria has brought a shoebox. It rests in her lap. She grips it tight.

"You're named in her will," I say. "Honora wanted you to have all her herbs and plant mixtures, the ones she keeps in her apothecary room."

Daria nods. I can't tell if she's pleased. She's lost in her thoughts.

"Sad thing, to be an old woman and watch a young woman like Honora die," she says finally.

"I found her. Dead," I say.

I wonder why I have just said such a thing so bluntly, so irreverently. When Diego died, no one stepped forward as the voyeur of his ugly dismissal. They had hidden their horror, probably out of a desire to protect the rest of us. Now I'm pitying myself, for no one worrying about me finding Honora nothing more than a carcass.

I'm no longer able to judge anyone based on the circumstances of their death, without having experienced who they had been, when living. I had experienced nothing of Diego's wisdom, because I hadn't even tried. I was too busy hiding.

When I glance over at Daria's face, I'm ashamed that she knows this.

"Ah, Andrea Anderson," Daria says. "Don't worry yourself over such a thing as seeing death, it will only haunt you. Death is nothing more than the price we pay for this privilege of having lived at all."

Daria straightens the taped box on her lap, sitting prim and alert in Honora's van. "When you were a kid, did you ever find a locust shell stuck to a tree branch? That hard covering with a neat slit up the back where the locust has climbed free?" she asks.

I think about this.

"Yes, I have."

"Did you take it from the tree bark, and hold it gently in your hand and marvel at it?"

"Yes, I did."

I think of Victor and me in the woods at the end of our cul-de-sac, focused on a paper-thin locust molt. Even its tiny pincers and its hair-strand legs had been encased in a brown crust. We'd been fascinated.

"You marveled at it," Daria continues, "because it was mysterious and unusual. But then you put it down, and you went back to playing. And that's the right thing to do."

I think of Honora. And Diego. Both dead, despite their private battles. Both leaving a unique legacy to be chosen by each of the people they had touched—including me, Andrea Anderson.

We drive in comfortable silence for a while. I notice the ordinariness of people. People who have not just lost Honora. People who wind garden hoses and run toy trucks along dirt paths in their driveways. People who unload groceries from the trunks of cars and shoot basketballs at hoops suspended from their garage doors.

But mostly, the driveways we pass have no one in them.

"Honora left Zena to me," I say at last. "I still have to ask my mom if I can keep her."

Daria weighs the solemnity of my voice, trying to tell if this is a big problem or a small one.

"Luckily, Zena is not a dog who is kept," she says. "She is a dog who owns people, not the other way around."

I nod.

"I'm going to find a way," I say.

"If it's meant to be, then you will make it so," Daria says. She reaches to pat my hand on the steering wheel. "But being owned by Zena is no small task."

I leave Daria off in the care of Hughie and Curtis, who

bustle around her with adoration. Before I close the door behind me, I hear Hughie suggesting a scalp massage.

"You poor dear, traveling in this heat," he says. "We'll pamper you and get you feeling lively in no time."

"I brought you boys some cookies," Daria says. "They're in a shoebox I put down around here somewhere." Hughie squeals with delight and I smirk. I tell Zena to stay as I close the door. Even though she has never made a move to leave with me after I've walked her, not once.

I go home in silence, wondering how to settle the matter of being owned by Zena.

Ashley's Mom-i-van is in the driveway when I get home.

Ashley's sitting on my couch with Mom and Gloria. She jumps to her feet, relieved, when I open the door.

"Andrea." Ashley hugs me and I feel myself flinch with surprise. "I heard what happened to Honora."

Gloria waves her skinny fingers in the air at us.

"Shame, really, that she didn't go into a hospice home," Gloria says. "Then poor Andrea here wouldn't have had to find her dead. Shocking thing for a teenager to go through, really."

I want to glare at Gloria. Instead, I smile. All the time I spent thinking about Diego and who found him rushes back to me. It's far from how that could have been. It wasn't horrific or terrifying. I know that Honora died content and it's comforting.

"Honora wanted to die at home," I say. "I wanted to help her do that."

Mom grunts.

"For seventy bucks a week, Andrea should have wiped her ass for her, too," Mom says. Ashley wilts with embarrassment.

I, however, do not.

I think of all the snide things my mom has done and

said, and how she doesn't really deserve to have Dennis love her. She doesn't really deserve to have me love her. She doesn't deserve to have Gloria. We all only cater to her out of desperation, out of a belief that she is as good as we deserve, too.

"You are so full of hate," I say. I look Mom right in the eyes. She says nothing.

Ashley is more than happy to follow me out the front door. We lean on the back bumper of her Mom-i-van.

"Boy, did I come over at a bad time." Ashley giggles softly.

"Pretty normal, actually," I say.

"Well, if that's normal, be sure to invite me to dinner sometime," Ashley says. "That would be a real kick in the ass."

"I'd rather invite you to dinner at the lightbulb oven in the gas station. They have a decent pizza there, if you catch it before it gets moldy."

"Well then, let's go." Ashley pops the car keys from her shorts pocket. I stare at the dashboard while she maneuvers out of our driveway. I don't want to look at my house. I wonder if Mom is seething inside, or if she and Gloria are eating potato chips and reading *TV Guide*.

6 Honora's funeral.

Ashley comes, and so do Roger Dupris and his mother. Mom and Dennis are there, and Gloria. There must be a hundred faces I don't recognize. Daria explains that many are her artist friends, a group of people that don't gather regularly, but seek each other out as kin in solemn times. I see James from Pocono Mountain Art, peering at the ceiling through his horn-rimmed glasses.

"Artists can be loners. It's a very solitary job," Daria says, her voice low in respect to the soprano banging out high notes in the balcony of the United Methodist Church of Simmonsville. "They come together to pay tribute to their own. Especially the tragic ones. Honora was so young."

Honora's obituary was in the paper yesterday. I found out she was forty. I also found out her husband had died before her. Gregory.

"How did her husband die, Daria?" I whisper.

"Car crash. Snowy roads. A chance meeting with a propane delivery truck."

"Did the accident happen at a crossroads?" I ask, smiling thinly.

"What?" says Daria.

The church is filled with the sound of rustling and discomfort. Ashley is sitting just behind Mom, who's sandwiched between Dennis and Gloria. Mom looks at me

251

bitterly, then leans into Gloria when I wave. She'd been annoyed when I told her that I'd been asked to do a reading, and that meant I had to sit in the front row. She'd been annoyed at my charcoal eyeliner and lace-up black boots. Ashley has lent me a straight black skirt that skims the tops of my boots, and I feel like I'm taller, like my top half has been carved from solid granite.

Ashley crosses her eyes at me and fans her face with Honora's mass card. She points vaguely to her own head, then to mine. Thumbs-up. She glances around to make sure no one has seen her and mistaken her gesture as being disrespectful.

"Just put a subtle little hint of emphasis on the part of you that is awkward, but smooth it out. Make it your quirk, your style, and don't be ashamed of it," Ashley had said as she rifled through her bedroom closet, considering blouses to go with the skirt. "Here," she said, offering me a crisp white top with a pointy collar.

"Very Addams Family," I say, wrinkling my nose. "So which of my awkward parts should I emphasize?"

"That's entirely up to you," Ashley had answered, cocking her hip to consider the blouse with the skirt with the boots with the Purple Rage nail polish.

Funny, we who live, how we behave at funerals. Some of us sit and evaluate the other mourners. We notice that someone owns a nice, tailored suit and someone else does not; we notice yellowed teeth and long-overdue haircuts. Some of us look at the church itself, and wonder about the people it has held over the years, mourning the loss of someone loved. We study the striations of the wood pew in front of us and the blue fleur-de-lis in stained glass. Some, a few, might consider the life of Honora, choosing random moments and never linking them together to sum up her story, because life isn't like that. It never ravels perfectly together and tightens into a finished work, polished by its artist and gazed upon by its admirers. Life is random, and its strands are individually beautiful—they don't need to bind together.

There's coughing and shuffling in the silence that follows a sharp crescendo on the church organ. The pastor appears and we stand, and there's talking. I don't listen. To listen means to acknowledge Honora's death, and I want self-preservation more than I want a tear-streamed face in public. I'm not convinced I can stop it, that I won't be revisited by that painful groan of loss, meant to be private.

Daria nudges me when it's my turn to go to the altar and read. My reading is on a folded piece of notebook paper. I glance at Dennis, who's the person I'd chosen to look at it first. He returns my gaze, expressionless.

Standing on the altar, I look out at the faces of Honora's friends. Possibly her family, too, though I wouldn't know any of them. Had a distant aunt driven down from Scranton with no pain, only a sense of duty? I might never know.

Many faces are curious, and I feel my heart flutter, because I'm suddenly certain I'll disappoint them. They'll lower their faces in disgust and pity when I'm finished.

They'll add one last memory to Honora's life—one about the odd girl who wrote a poem to read at her funeral, and performed miserably.

Then I see Mom looking at me nervously, like I might embarrass her by acting like a fool. I unfold my paper and put my cheek near the microphone.

Live like you are extraordinary.
Love like you admire someone's most painful burden.
Breathe like the air is scented with lavender and fire.
See like the droplets of rain are each exquisite.
Laugh like the events of existence are to be cherished.
Imagine like there is magic in your fingertips.
Give freedom to your instincts, to your spirit, to your
*   longing.*

No one seems particularly impressed at the end of my reading, until I look at Hughie and Daria. Dennis and Ashley. They're all beaming, and Hughie is dabbing his eyelashes with a folded Kleenex. And that is enough for me. I'm understood, if only by a few. It's enough.

Mom is staring into her lap. I wonder if she listened.

Honora's casket, set in front of the altar so that I must walk past it on the way back to my seat, looks small. I smile when I look at the fabric that's been draped over it, by Hughie himself. It's an Inuit-print blanket from northern Canada, bought for Honora by her dead husband years ago. Inside, I know Honora's head has been wrapped in an indigo-blue African headpiece that looks fabulous with her multicolored caftan from Greece. Hughie laughed until he cried when he told Curtis and me about the funeral home director's face, as he unwrapped the garments Honora had chosen.

"I love it," he gasped. "This ultraconservative pasty-faced repressionist, with his eyes bugged out of his head. Very professional, though, didn't say a word about it. Oh, to be a fly on the wall inside that guy's skull. Honora loved to surprise people, that's for sure."

When I sit down, Daria pats my knee and settles back for the rest of the ceremony. My heart slowly eases its pounding, and I count the candles on the altar and admire my black clubfeet. My feet are sweating, but this betrayal is concealed tightly inside.

Everyone mills around the parking lot after Honora's casket is slid into the back of the hearse.

Ashley is standing with Roger Dupris and his mother. Mrs. Dupris smiles at me when I approach.

"Andrea, you just keeping growing up," she says. Roger flinches with embarrassment.

"Thanks, Mrs. Dupris." I give Roger a patient, knowing smile. Been there, too, but it could be worse.

"It's hot again, just like at Mr. Diego's thing," Mrs. Dupris goes on. "Why don't the three of you take an hour and jump in the pool at our house?"

"Um, I don't even own a swimsuit," I say.

"I've got spares," Ashley says, more to Mrs. Dupris than to me. "Roger and I have to work at five, so how's two o'clock?"

Both Roger and Mrs. Dupris smile in delight.

"We'll see you girls at two."

"I hate you," I hiss at Ashley when the Duprises leave.

"Good. You'll be so filled with hate for me, you won't have any left in you to hate my swimsuits," Ashley hisses back. "I'll come at one-thirty so you have time to try a few on."

"If you even think about showing up with a bikini," I threaten. Then Ashley notices Mom and Dennis coming toward us, and makes a getaway through the crowd.

256

Dennis pats my shoulder and Mom crosses her arms, glaring at me.

"So, I understand there is the matter of this dog," she says.

"Hughie and I spoke," Dennis offers by way of apology. "He and Curtis have to go back home today. The dog thing needs to be addressed."

I wonder, briefly, what it would be like to have Mom in my court, on my side, instead of always having her as my opponent.

Dennis's shirt is sweat-stained across the top of his belly.

I try to read him for a clue as to what angle I need to take with the dog thing. Should I plead? Should I tell her how I will pay for every need and desire of Zena myself, with the money I saved up from Honora, and the job I will try to get at Gimelli's Shop and Run? That I had already accepted Daria's offer of forty dollars to take her bowls to galleries once a month, splitting the money with Ashley so we could use her Mom-i-van?

In the silence that weighs heavy between us, I look away. We're each statues, isolated in our own bodies. Me in my solid black boots, Dennis with his sweat stains, and Mom with her venom glare.

People are drifting toward cars, some laughing. Others are gathered in circles, lamenting their loss. Gloria is in a group with Hughie, Curtis, and Daria, offering directions on how to get back to the main road from here. She is reveling in their attention, even if it's only about driving directions.

"You know we can't keep that huge dog," Mom says. My eyes meet hers, which are straining at their limits to stare me down to a sniveling earthworm writhing in the hot sun, there in front of Honora's hearse.

Dennis coughs lightly into his fist, and looks away.

Mom and I are standing on either side of a ravine, eying each other from the boundaries of our relationship, that distant meeting place for people who don't really understand each other. We're stubborn and different. In a face-off, I've been at a disadvantage my whole life. How could I, when I was pitted against a woman who never let me win?

"Zena is mine," I whisper, refusing to let my eyes waver from hers. "And I belong to Zena. There is no other way."

There's an edge of pleading in my voice, something I didn't want there, something I had fought to control. My sweat spreads across the soles of my feet. But I hold my face fierce.

"Honora's friends are such interesting people." Gloria is suddenly at Mom's elbow. She smiles in sweet hopeful-ness at me. She does not acknowledge the tension that is suffocating me, and I feel like Gloria is a ghostly figure in a room, looking startled to find it changed.

"Shall we go back to your place for a glass of wine?"

Mom lowers her stare and glances at Gloria.

"You should have heard the nice things they said about Andrea," Gloria continues. "Apparently that dog is a good one. That poet guy called her a Majesty Queen or some-thing."

"A majestic beast," I whisper. "I bet he called her a majestic beast."

Mom snorts.

"A majestic pain in the ass, with majestic crap all over the lawn," Mom says.

"Oh," says Gloria. She ponders her nail polish job, then sighs.

"What about that girlfriend of yours, Andrea?" Gloria says. "You said her family has dogs. Would they take Zena?"

"No," I answer.

From the corner of my eye I see Dennis loosen the neck button of his shirt. I glance at him, and he winks at me so briefly, I almost miss it. He is done benchwarming.

"Yeah, but Ashley could tell Andrea where to take the dog to the vet. And I bet she'd walk it if Andrea couldn't for some reason, right?"

"Yes," I answer meekly. I'm ready for Dennis to take a round.

"Plus, you always worry about Andrea being home alone when we go out bowling or to the movies. She's old enough to be home by herself all night, if we went away.

"That is, if she had Zena. We could go to a couple of those antique shows in the Poconos this fall."

Mom's face flickers. The woman whose upper lip curled into a snarl when I entered a room, who was able to squash my hopes with her hard disdain, looks at Dennis, and then at me. Her face has an unusual expression. Like maybe she thought when Dennis moved in, he would stop caring about her. But here he was, planning trips with her, solving her worries.

And for the first time in my life that I can think of, my Mom's expression looks hopeful.

8 I go with Ashley to the Duprises' house at two. Roger's skimming the pristine pool with a net. Ashley's donated swimsuits, four in total, had all looked strange on me. I had chosen the one least out of character, a black tank that's a little baggy in the chest.

"A couple of the guys are coming over, too." Roger glances at Ashley, as if he's afraid she'll dislike this development. Ashley shrugs.

One of the guys turns out to be a basketball player who has cast doubtful glances at me from Roger's driveway. The other is Wendy Cartwright's little brother, Paul. They steal furtive glances at Ashley, who's sitting at the edge of the pool, dangling her tan legs in the turquoise water.

"Hey," offers Paul.

"Hey," Ashley says back. She slides into the pool without flinching. Roger dives precisely into the deep end and surfaces.

"Come on in, Andrea," Ashley urges. I shoot her an anguished scowl.

The basketball player and Paul cannonball into the pool, carefully avoiding Ashley. Ashley is meeting my scowl with her own, like she is willing me not to be ashamed, not to be disliked. I meet her halfway in her stubbornness to get me to come alive, and walk to the edge of the pool and hunker down.

"I'll just dangle my feet in," I say.

"The hell you will!" Ashley grabs my wrists and yanks. I feel a moment of horror as I flail forward. Then I'm underwater, in a tangle with Ashley, both of us struggling to surface.

Ashley comes up laughing. I come up sputtering and gasping. I feel wonderful and offended, all at once. Ashley has rivulets of pool water running down her face into her open mouth. She yanks my wrists beneath the surface of the water and I squirm to be freed from her grasp. We surface again, laughing.

I know then that Ashley has become my best friend.

Afterward, Paul and I are lying in poolside chairs and watching Ashley tie her towel around her waist. I'm wary of Paul. I know he's cruel.

"I think it's going to storm," Ashley says to us when she notices we've been watching her.

"God, I hope so," I answer, and arrange the straps on my borrowed bathing suit before deciding I don't care if they look good or not.

The color of the sky has gone lavender, with an ominous green-black clot to the west of Roger's backyard moving in our direction. The five of us stretch out in beach chairs and watch.

There's a moment when the birds and insects pause,

as if taking a collective breath. Then the humidity lifts away in a flutter that makes the hair on my arms rise.

"It's going to be a good one," Paul says.

Thunder has begun to gather strength.

"Why don't you kids come inside?" Mrs. Dupris calls from the back screen door. We all ignore her. Spasms of lightning are collecting in the darkest part of the cloud. The leaves in Roger's yard start rustling in anticipation.

A thunderclap nearby makes me jump.

"Nature is pretty amazing," Paul says.

I'm surprised to discover he's talking to me.

When the rain comes, we remain in the lounge chairs and allow the downpour to pelt our bodies. We don't speak.

I think of Honora, of the pottery I had thought I destroyed in the rain. I think about the charred ruins of her work, on the workbench in her cobblestone shed.

Everyone thinks the phoenix rises from the ashes, gleaming and unscathed. Until they know better.

And now I think I understand what she meant.

I smile and let grateful tears gather in my eyes, let them run down my cheeks and get lost in the rainwater. *Thank you, Honora.*

I think of Victor, my first best friend. I think of Ashley and Dennis, Hughie and Daria, and even Roger Dupris. All these people my friends. Not one of them alike; each one extraordinary and fascinating like the glazes Honora had painted her pottery with. None the exact shade of either light or darkness, but instead some degree between the two. Each possessed beauty beneath the surface.

Maybe even Paul did, too.

Mom is watching reruns of *Petticoat Junction* when I get home.

"Don't sit on that chair if you're wet," she commands, fiddling with her remote control.

"I'm not wet," I say.

Mom glances at me.

"Well, then don't sit in that chair when you're supposed to be out buying a chain and hook for the back porch. You're going to have to tie that beast outside when she gets on my nerves."

I wait. I wait for her to yank it back, to extinguish the offer of hope. I know it can happen, so I wait.

Mom almost outwaits me. Then she tosses me her car keys and releases the pause button.

"You can drive my car. Try to figure that piece of junk out. Lord knows, I can't," she says.

The keys land on the floor at my feet, and I look at them for several moments before I pick them up.

265

10 "Oh, thank heavens you've come for Zena," Hughie says. "Thank heavens that worked out right."

Hughie and Curtis have neat, rectangular suitcases set side by side at the front door. Daria has a half-zipped duffle bag and a drawstring Peruvian bag propped against each other nearby.

"We're dropping off darling Daria on our way back home," Hughie says. "We had two final matters of business, and your arrival has taken care of them both."

Curtis hands Hughie an envelope. Its front has Honora's scrawly handwriting. *Daria, Hughie, Curtis, and Andrea.* The ink is lavender, and I smile.

"You should open it, Daria," Hughie says.

Daria unseals the envelope with a gnarled finger and slides out a carefully folded letter.

Daria, Hughie, Curtis, and Andrea,
I only ask that my ashes be spread
By you, my dearest of friends,
In the Adirondack Mountains
Where my only flesh and blood on this earth continue
To see the wonders of this fascinating world.

I think of Honora, many centuries from now, a pebble lodged in the crevice of a mountain cliff. Or a pliant, sturdy wisp of weed, clinging to a small patch of dirt. Or a deer contently navigating a snow-covered mountain path. Or a raven perched in the highest branch of a wind-beaten pine tree.

"I've always enjoyed a good road trip," Daria says after a thoughtful moment. "It was Honora herself who said it opened the mind to new senses."

"Ladies and gents, I believe we're about to embark on a road trip to the north, in final honor of Honora." Hughie has clasped his hands together, his mind already scrutinizing the logistics of getting the four of us to the Adirondacks.

"A mountain, rising perpendicular to a chilly, dark lake. That's how Honora described it," Daria says, adjusting the buckles on her sandals. "Blue Mountain Lake. I recall the name because she named a pottery glaze after it."

"Is that where her son lives?" I ask.

"Oh, no, dear. It's where her husband took her for their first anniversary. She fell in love with it.

"As for the son, Honora asked us to mail him a letter when she died. That's all. None of us read it, it was sealed. Curtis put it out this morning. Honora would not have wanted her ashes to be spread right on top of him. Near him is all she wanted. And *near* is such a relative term."

"How near is Blue Mountain Lake to him?" I ask.

"Many rocks, rivers, streams, and mountains away," Daria smiles. "Zena must make the trip, too, of course." She pats Zena's head.

"Shall we go next weekend?" Hughie asks.

The night before we leave for the Adirondacks, I curl up in my bed.

I face our street with the window open wide.

Zena is on the floor, the kitten curled against her barrel-like chest. Zena, the squirrel-chaser, had politely sniffed Hefty upon their introduction. The kitten had fallen in love. So had Dennis.

"That's a trained dog," Dennis had said to me, watching Zena settle on the carpet and politely endure Hefty's ill-mannered claws on her tail. "A real beauty, too."

Even Mom had unsnarled her lip during Zena's well-behaved inspection of the kitchen trash can.

"Mom?" I said.

"Uh-huh."

"Thanks. For letting her stay."

Mom had looked surprised. Just like the look she had given Dennis at Honora's funeral when he helped me gain permission to be owned by Zena. Like there's still a chance for something unexplored to blossom between us, not the grim expectation of disappointment.

At that moment, I realized what Mom and Dennis shared—hope. Simple hope.

It was something we all deserved.

"You've wanted a dog for a long time, Andrea," Mom had said. "You used to ask me for one, remember?"

Ashley had stopped by long enough to bury her face in Zena's neck and tell her how beautiful she was.

"Andrea's going to bring you to the park. Maybe you can be Kooky's girlfriend," Ashley had cooed in Zena's ear. Now Zena and I are silent in my dark bedroom. We are both listening to the baritone rumble of thunder. Tomorrow we'll say farewell to Honora. We, her friends, will cast her ashes into a distant lake, where the particles of Honora will travel, forever lost to us. But each of us had the gifts bestowed by Honora, friendship and acceptance and hope. We had lived a space of our own lives in the presence of a beautiful person—a woman who was imperfect, but content. A woman who saw each of us as the colors in the palette of her life, who saw beauty lying beneath the surface of ordinary people, like me. *Andrea Anderson, you are this and so much more.*

Honora was right.

It's all in the lighting, what we see. I know now that I am an artist. I can guide myself toward my own version of art and beauty. Just by exploring what's inside my own head. And seeing other people as prisms held up to the sun, each angle different, depending on the perception of the onlooker.

I think again of Honora, guiding my hand with her paintbrush, encouraging me to take the time to see the delayed perception of color.

It's a wonderful sensation if you allow yourself the time it takes to experience it.

From the floor, Zena raises her massive head to listen to

the thunder. Her silhouette is reassuring to me. I can hear Mom and Dennis downstairs, picking out duplicates from their now-combined CD collection, laughing at each other's taste in music.

When lightning flashes, I can see a burst of brilliance over the darkness of the world.

Then it goes dark again.

ACKNOWLEDGMENTS

I am grateful for those who have helped make *Skin Deep* happen: the YA contest selection committee at Delacorte Press; editor Krista Marino for her intuition, guidance, and encouragement; Mark for both the gift of his art and the help on how to convey it in words; Mia for being my personal cheerleader; Lyn for being my BFR (Brave First Reader); KK for being the seed for this story; and the family and friends who make life an adventure worth writing about, because you never know where it will take you.

© GORDON W. PERKINS

E. M. CRANE is the winner of the 2006 Delacorte Press Contest for a First Young Adult Novel. She lives with her husband and daughter in Sackets Harbor, New York, where she is a full-time writer. *Skin Deep* is her first book for young adults.